OPHIR

OPHIR

Swords, Ciphers & the DM Code

ANDREW DAVID DOYLE

Copyright © 2021 by Andrew David Doyle.

Library of Congress Control Number: 2021906567

PAPERBACK: 978-1-955347-13-6
EBOOK: 978-1-955347-14-3

All rights reserved. No part of this publication may be reproduced, distributed, or transmitted in any form or by any electronic or mechanical means, without the prior written permission of the publisher, except in the case of brief quotations embodied in critical reviews and certain other noncommercial uses permitted by copyright law.

Ordering Information:

For orders and inquiries, please contact:
1-888-404-1388
www.goldtouchpress.com
book.orders@goldtouchpress.com

Printed in the United States of America

CONTENTS

Acknowledgements..vii
Dedication ix
Characters xi
Foreword...xiii

Chapter 1   'Characters & Codes'...1
Chapter 2   'The Shugborough Inscription'..................................6
Chapter 3   'Kemp Hastings' 18
Chapter 4   'Visitors' 25
Chapter 5   'DM Code'...34
Chapter 6   'The Literal Context: The Arcadian Shepherd' 40
Chapter 7   'Nicolas Poussin's real genius'................................46
Chapter 8   'DM - 1696' 51
Chapter 9   'Hastings and the Admiralty'.................................58
Chapter 10 'Rumbo'l Dumpling'..76
Chapter 11 'The Seventh lamp'..86
Chapter 12 'The Cockpit' 97
Chapter 13 'The Business end of Piracy'................................102
Chapter 14 'Inkychung – Madagascar'...................................110
Chapter 15 'Guests of Dishonour' 112
Chapter 16 'St Mary's Isle' 120
Chapter 17 'The Avon Ascoti' 124

Chapter 18 'Ophir – Solomon's Ethiopia' 130
Chapter 19 'Kidd's Eternal Grave' 136
Chapter 20 'The Demise of the Avon Ascoti' 146
Chapter 21 'The Sword dedicated to William the IIIrd' 152
Chapter 22 'Telescope' 157
Chapter 23 'The Horseshoe Expedition' 162
Chapter 24 'Santa Clara Island' 166

Afterword 173
Author Biography 177

ACKNOWLEDGEMENTS

I would like to acknowledge the wonderful people below for allowing me to hijack important parts of their intimate psyche and character make up; it is without such personalities that novel stories would never come alive as they should and my gratitude is extended to them and also to the great historical figures captured within global media networks such as Google and Wikipedia, which has facilitated access to many platforms and archives.

This novel is a fictitious piece of work and the literature reviews and online research has allowed the author to interrogate a great deal of empirical knowledge, albeit remains cognisant that in order to write such a novel fact and fiction has been merged together to create the timeline where some key events may have or may have not occurred at all.

DEDICATION

This novel is dedicated to:

Mr. Ed Hill and his spouse of many years, Stella Hill, who hail from Dundee in Scotland where this novel evolves from. A testament to a life-long partnership in marriage.

CHARACTERS

Mister Manoj Dhimal – Saudi Arabia
Mister Narinder Sudanini – Saudi Arabia

Historical

Captain William Kidd Deceased
Admiral Adam Duncan Deceased
Lord George Anson Deceased
Explorer Juan Fernandez Deceased
Don Juan Estaban De Ubilla y Echeverria Deceased

FOREWORD

Imagine a world where treasure seekers, pirates, and the landed gentry, including royalty from across several continents, had got involved in the clandestine world of murder, piracy, deception, and espionage, where these institutions were suddenly having to be made accountable for their actions and treachery. Well, that would be a fine result, albeit this novel and work of fiction is not aimed at that particular purpose. This work captures many such elements, albeit the crux of this narrative is who knew what? And who deceived who? Especially when such deception involved the riches of King Solomon and the Inca's and involved some unscrupulous perpetrators that have unceremoniously tread upon some serious Christian toes, including the Knights Templar, to achieve their evil ends. To set forth on this journey of discovery, we shall start with the most obvious secret code of the 16th and 17th century where this story revolves around and we should declare this also involves the elusive DM Code. And as we work our way through the many pieces of fact and fiction whilst flirting in the footsteps of some rather amazing swash buckling scoundrels, we will also touch on certain aspects that may or may not be known to a wider audience, or certain details may even not be true at all. However, these notions and ideas are brought together for an amazing set of adventures that are designed to stimulate readers and scholars alike for many years to come, especially when great wealth is in the offering. This work, therefore, is not designed to answer the DM Code nor any other codes or conundrums mentioned in the work to any academic level, albeit the author has drawn from many sources of knowledge that have triggered key elements that should inspire readers to think about the acts of piracy and the very nature of serious deception that have in fact taken the many lives of both the innocent and guilty people over the centuries. The key focus of this adventure is based on the characters: Captain William Kidd, Lord George Anson, General Esteban Ubilla, Explorer Juan Fernandez, and not dismissing Captain Cornelius Webb.

The overall time frame for this work steps back and forth through short periods as snapshots to accommodate the inclusion of these colourful characters as we start to discover in life the scant details which outline one of the many early meanings of the DM Code itself. The author intimates that there are several conclusions or solutions to this elusive code and does not profess to have solved the great riddle with any definitive standing but poses a narrative that should make certain establishments sit up and take careful note of how treacherous life at sea actually was, especially during the 15th to the 17th centuries. Although the author has conducted a fair degree of research into some of the speculation and spurious conditions regarding the actual Horseshoe Expedition, which was allegedly managed under the directions of Lord George Anson or the British Admiralty prior to Anson's death in 1762, the caveat also presented is that this clandestine project may also have been just a clever ploy of misdirection and that the real outcome of the DM Code may well still be lurking somewhere in Arcadia in Greece as opposed to being attached to a more dynamic naval search for great riches in the South Pacific, or was a notion simply attached to a physical account of intrigue and grand theft. However, for the art and sake of amazing storytelling and perhaps subtle stimulation of the work, the reader is also reminded that great wealth still remains to be discovered deep within the ocean waters of our beautiful planet or can still be found buried on the many islands that were indeed used by pirates and ancient warlords of yesteryear to hide their unfathomable ill-gotten wealth. Therefore, in order to engage the world at large, we need to take a look at some pieces of so-called evidence for inspirational purposes, and to begin with, we shall dwell on the infamous Shepherd's inscription or the infamous Templar code as it is often referred to by scholars from across many disciplines, where we will discover that since its advent the depiction of the work has been a certain puzzle for the world academic community to consider. This Shugborough conundrum as an example has the dreamers of the world reeling at their desks and drooling over their catalogues and books, crouching over their technical laptops; and they will respond if asked? What is the real DM Code all about?

A normal retort is that this is a potential road map to the secret society of the Knights Templar's hidden treasure and they collectively may of course be correct in their assumptions, or the more loving and compassionate amongst us will say that it is simply a memorial message to a dearly loved departed spouse, but the sceptical and demanding of society will say that they agree with the conspiracy theorists who collectively state that the Priory of Sion are telling the informed world at large that the 'Holy Grail' is not too far away from reality and that the Knights Templar are the current custodians of such important relics. Therefore, it comes with absolute certainty and no surprise, however, where we can say without any doubt that this particular subject has quite literally baffled the historical, academic, and scientific communities for many decades and such is the nature of the conundrum that in its wake many exciting novels and fantastical academic papers have been written and presented to address the myriad of fanciful ideas and notions put forward to solve Anson's ingenious legacy. With that in mind, there have also been many variations as to what Admiral George Anson was actually hiding or indeed secreting as to what his real intention was when he concocted the code, if, in fact, he had engineered the inscription in the first place, and, therefore, without resistance offers some juicy subject matter for great debate to the world as to what he was actually alluding to when his brother, Thomas Anson, built the rustic arch and shrine under specific instructions between the years 1748 - 1763.

The question being asked currently is: Was there ever an overarching interpretation or a written explanation or record captured on vellum or was it really only the shepherd's monument that was to hold the true secret of Shugborough hall? And today we find that the 'shepherds monument' is without any challenge to its existence reflected in respect to Nicolas Poussin's interpretation of the 'Et in arcadia ego' paintings, which has had several minor changes to the actual bas relief erected within the arch at Shugborough, and when this elegant work is viewed or compared against the original Poussin artwork, one can observe certain subtle differences. Although we should acknowledge that (Poussin painted two interpretations of the same event) and our attention is therefore drawn firstly to the raised solid bas relief being the third part of the clandestine project as it came much later into existence though it may still make no reference as to the real question of why. Some of these changes were incorporated and clearly differed from the two original paintings. An example being the elevation of the fingers of the right hand from the shepherd who is kneeling before the shepherdess and pointing specifically to the letter 'R' in the inscription. If we wish to delve deeper, one could also involve secret geometry and that will take the reader into the realms of discovering the art of mystery or enlightenment of perhaps highlighting the symbol regarding 'Vesica Piscia' regarding the shepherdess and her pose, which will certainly create a map or diagram that could and would eventually lead back to the Priory of Sion and to yet another conundrum in the form of a Latin text to be deciphered, which can be found on their 'POS seal and the letters to decipher are – 'I Tego arcana dei' (Begone – I concern the secrets of God). To this end and to keep the flow of this narrative, the adventure within these pages should remain in the maritime domain for good reason and the overall influences of several sources of information from more than a few obscure sources may have been absorbed and included in the text, albeit included into the work with no intent to engineer or capture their presence as the Priory of Sion into the narrative. And the author presents his thoughts that other interpretations of this great conundrum should be kept in the domain of the Greek gods such as Athens and Pan.

The real rationale and explanation as to why these changes were made by Anson must have been executed for a very good reason indeed and perhaps that fact and mystery is only for George Anson himself or the Admiralty to answer. The **S**toryline covers many aspects that evolved in and around the lives of George Anson, Captain William Kidd, and other historical figures from history in the passing, including royalty and a few people of notoriety from the 18th century. The notation below emerged in 1762 and certainly alludes to the secret that may or may not be held within the fabric of the DM code and clearly points in the direction of Shugborough Hall, the ancestral home of the Anson family, as a reference point. Parliamentary reading 1762 at the time of death of George Anson.

> "Upon that storied marble cast thine eye
> The scene commands a moralising sigh
> E'en in Arcadia's bless'd **Elysian** plains
> Amidst the laughing nymphs and sportive swains
> See festal joy subside, with melting grace
> And pity visit the half smiling face;
> Where now the dance, the lute, the nuptial feast
> The passion throbbing in the lover's breast
> Life's emblem here, in youth and vernal bloom
> But **reason's** finger pointing at the tomb!"

CHAPTER ONE

'Characters & Codes'

'Ophir' – *Biblical*

> 'A maritime port mentioned in the Bible, a place famous for the movement of great riches of King Solomon. Kings 10:22. 'Fruitful or bountiful place of riches' name derivation - 'Ofir' ancient name port of Ofir - located in Ethiopia'

Kemp Hastings and the Holy Order had an entirely different agenda on their hands to deliver than that of the British Navy who were currently engaged in raping and pillaging the high seas for great wealth in their drive for power and greed for the empire, and had embarked on a scheme of privateering and deliberate orchestrated plunder at sea to appease the monarch of the day King William the IIIrd. To this end and unknown to the crown, the British privateers and British Navy vessels had attacked and looted a single vessel that was important to the Holy Order of the Knights Templar, and Britain was about to be held accountable for their actions and have their proverbial fingers slapped and severely burnt as a simple warning. Kemp Hasting was a young naval officer and had been given a secret plan, which to execute was a 'task' set by the order to undertake in the strictest of confidence. It was also to be operating under clear directions from the Holy Order's representative and was given details of a master plan, which in essence meant securing the signature pieces of Christendom, including the infamous wealth of King Solomon, which accumulated as a hoard of wealth known as the 'Ophir riches', which formed part of a haul plundered from the merchant shipping vessel whilst it was sailing on the high seas in and around the lands of Egypt, India, and Ethiopia. This particular theft, however, had triggered one of the most unlikely relationships ever to be forged during very uncertain times and became an undocumented partnership between the infamous Captain William Kidd and a Knight of the Holy Order Naval Lieutenant Kemp Hastings who had both found themselves thrown together under unprecedented circumstances and were quite literally bound together in Christian duty, each having made a solemn promise to deliver on their bond and formed a partnership that was to become a pact that neither of them fully understood nor could ever fathom in their wildest of dreams or had ever considered as a possibility regarding the secret world that they were about to enter.

It was a domain where these two crusaders would walk blindly into, the strange world of mass deception and piracy on the high seas, where theft, murder, and general skull-duggery were commonplace. Kemp Hastings having already been recruited by the Knights of Santiago in early 1667 was commissioned to trace the known whereabouts of a British pirate vessel that was involved in this grand theft and was rumoured that the ship could still be carrying the holy relics and artifacts; these were important holy relics that cemented the foundation and belief of the Judaic, Christian and Muslim faiths together. It was in those earlier days Hastings had found himself traversing the globe as a sea-rover or mariner with two of his closest companions who had been cast adrift in the oceans and had been found drifting at sea for almost six days and were lucky enough to have been rescued by the crew of the Frigate '**HMS Fortuna**' and its seasoned officer, Captain Will Irons, who took the men on board the vessel with open arms and helped Hastings to forge his new career as a new age mariner. It was only after a few years as a sea-rover that Hastings eventually found himself as First Officer acting with a naval commission and operating within the Admiralty that led to his chance encounter with his folly and had been inadvertently assigned to the very vessel that he had been tracking and attempting to locate for a long time, the '**HMS Wager**'. In a written Hebrew text that was presented to him earlier in his life by the Holy Order Hastings was tasked to locate the 'oni' of King Solomon—'oni' meaning 'ship'—and was informed that the text he held on his person was a reliable source of information extracted from an ancient text concerning King Hiram and involved the potential discovery of many great riches, and his quest was to find it, and that was about all that he knew at the time, but more importantly, the order had referenced a map with the sea routes that should be taken in order to receive the 'Ofir' of great wealth. Before this point, Hastings had been a wanderer for several years prior and was part of an archaeology team living and working near the port of Jaffa in Jordan before he joined a British merchant ship crew as a sea-rover and was working his way back to his homeland in Scotland when his colleague was attacked and murdered, leaving a small pack of personal belongings and some documents behind him. It was during the quick burial that the Knights had found and approached Hastings and had passed on the duty of locating 'Ofir' to him. He had provided the scant details of a special holy relic and that this was his duty to God and was to follow the trade routes into Ethiopia. The information provided basically stated that King Solomon's ships travelled from 'Tarshish' to 'Ophir' in Ethiopia frequently carrying great cargo and were carrying great wealth. In the modern-day circa 1270, The Knights Templar had carried this mantle of succession and continued this holy tradition to secure the transition of wealth between the port Ofir and the Kingdom of Solomon in the Middle East using the port of Tyre and Jaffa as their operating bases.

At some point, there was an attack regarding an unmarked Templar vessel which had been intercepted and several important ancient maps had also been stolen by 'unknown' pirates whilst the vessel the 'Temple Unicorn I' was en-route towards Ethiopia. Hastings like many other sharp-minded sailors knew about the life of the Queen of Sheba and the great riches of Ethiopia and he had also embarked on a journey in her footsteps that would be recorded in his personal journals as the **Ophir Expedition;** well, at least as far as he was concerned it was. And as history recently revealed there are many great riches still waiting to be discovered in the big wide world. However, the real riches of Solomon or the gold of the Incas is the proverbial icing on the cake and has always been on the radar for treasure hunters for decades to discover, and great stories of expeditions had been stemming up through the centuries, accompanied with some key historical characters along with maps and elusive codes, some of which are highlighted below and are just another addition to the human inventory who understood hidden codes coupled with their colourful characters that have taken their rightful places in the history of the 'Ophir'.

'George Anson' 1697 – 1762

George Anson Admiral of the Fleet, 1st Baron Anson, PC FRS, was a Royal Navy officer. Anson served as a junior officer during the War of the Spanish Succession and then saw active service against Spain ...But had gone to find the 'Horseshoe' riches.

'Nicolas Poussin'- 1594 - 1665

Nicolas Poussin was an artist famed for many great paintings and had been attributed to the masterpieces that may hold the keys as to where some very significant holy relics and treasures may or may not be located. 'Les bergers d'Arcadia' - The Arcadian Shepherds

'William Kidd' 1645 – 1701

William Kidd, Captain, Scottish sailor, Dundee/Glasgow and hailed as one of the most infamous pirates of the high seas, justly or unjustly so, Kidd was a man who was eventually arrested and trialled under a political rule that was to become utterly shambolic, after which William Kidd was put to death as he protected a great secret and very important pieces of treasure and wealth beyond imagination, the trove known as the **Cara** that was hidden near Catalina 1697.

Albeit the Captain was criminalised by the lack of support from his Government backers and the lack of supporting evidence and documents, e.g.: (Letter of Marque) that were deliberately hidden out of sight during the shambolic trial, which would, in reality, have exonerated William Kidd from said charges, but sadly, the trial was designed for only one outcome. (Orchestrated State Murder). The crux of the trial and hanging sentence was eventually based on the murder of Gunner William Moore, which was indeed a tragic accident. Although had Captain Kidd at some point really also known about the existence of the Explorer Juan Fernandez and his Inca treasure - which eventually fell into the possession of one General Juan Esteban Ubilla - Knights of Santiago, then at a later date the Society of London under Captain Webb and Lord Anson.

'Kemp Hastings' 1645 - 1745

Kemp Hastings – Knights Templar RL, Royal Lodge, Mariner R.N. and mercenary. Hailed from Dundee as a mariner and emigrated to the West indies circa 1680, and joined forces with Captain W. Kidd at various stages of his intrepid naval life up until circa 1700, in order to undertake a quest of the utmost importance.

CHAPTER TWO

'The Shugborough Inscription'

Cypher - *noun: 'a method of encryption or decryption'*

The Captain's official vessel's log book sat in full view to the casual observer sitting on top of the old officer's flat-topped wooden sea chest. The ship's log was already open at page thirty-three where the pages were virtually being held apart by the use of a small golden crucifix attached to a rather lengthy piece of the very elaborate golden chain. This particular lucky charm having been strategically laid neatly in the fold of the two pages was rather elegant. This highly recognisable symbol and icon of the Christian faith had been tethered together by a lashing of very ornate interwoven golden linked chain with two small golden acorns at each end of the tail pieces, which were draped across inside the ledger, with only a few inches dropping down over the side of the finely woven end of the brown leather dustcover. The log book appeared to be a normal insignificant register on the surface in its make up at first sight, but, in reality, this was quite different internally from its original or intended use and layout as required by the Royal Navy of the day. Suffice to say that apart from the register's very well constructed and very elaborate thick leather cover binding it, it would be literally quite difficult to tell average ledgers apart.

The spine of the log appeared to be very highly decorated with traces of interspersed Latin or Greek symbols, coupled with strong bold lettering which had been inlaid with a flashing of an intricate example of expensive gold leaf boldly splashed over the outer surface, but more specifically to the observer, two large bold letters stamped the authority of the owner of this register and highlighted the simple fact that this book was deemed important to someone and those letters were the initials - G.A. clearly embossed on the façade of the cover. The ledger's many loose internal fly sheets were also very well constructed, and one could observe that around the peripheral edges of the pages, there was a series of gilded lettering in an elongated cartouche denoting the name of George Anson coupled with the family's crest, the insignia clearly visible by each letter and symbol having been neatly and very competently etched into the soft skin of the leather hide. The larger protective outer dust jacket was more of a toughened type of vellum and a person would think that the dust jacket itself was made from either manta ray or even shark skin, (a trait often used in China for protective coverings for varying articles, including war materials or fighting (armour), but it was fully accepted by academics that the choice of leather for the binding of normal maritime books of this 'era' was the norm, and was very much adopted in this part of the world. To the casual observer, however, this example was simply stating that 'Anson' was somehow either very different in his character and had adopted a style of operating quite differently from most other Captains of his time were, or conversely that he was simply working under the assumption that his voyages were somehow more important than any typical or general planned Navy expedition, or the most obvious case of all was that Captain George Anson was simply operating within the realm of His Majesty's most secretive Admiralty department.

The wooden carry case that contained the ledger was also quite extraordinary in its overall construction and design as the top cover or lid was itself embossed with another very recognisable insignia of the infamous Anson family crest, of which, again the inlay was clearly visible and boldly etched into the fine wooden inlay with an additional lashing of expensive decoration etched in ivory with many tiny silver crosses and Christian symbols etched deep within the wooden frame.

The box being the protective external carry case for the elegant book, but nevertheless, it was still a simple ledger. Or was it? Of course, in Naval terms, some of these protective cases also protected some very highly detailed accounts of sea voyages with important entries indeed, and often they would contain secret information or accounts regarding the day to day activities, which would be actual maritime historical events and were certainly used as physical legal evidence should the need arise and were often employed as crucial evidence to either 'hang' a pirate or mutineer, or conversely, be employed as protective cases for housing War Orders or 'Orders' from the Crown. Albeit, it was not unusual for these entries to be reviewed at important trials or cases before the condemned were sent to execution dock at Wapping to serve their deathly sentence as was Captain William Kidd. But, for George Anson, this particular register was a highly secretive detailed account of a very private arrangement and covered a wide range of recordings regarding several undisclosed or secret voyages.

In recent days, many unscheduled sailings chartered by the East India Company were becoming a concern as they were starting to move a great deal of commercial value across the open seas, and collectively they had decided not to be so transparent with their global partners, and as a direct result across the pond in old London town in 17th century England, the Navy was becoming ever so worried as they had somehow lost their lucrative grip on international trade. But even more so with five of their newest ships having been recently attacked by those nasty pirates. Hence, why a clutch of Master Mariners had started to keep the details of their voyages ultra-secret. These were Journey's so secretive that even the crown may not have been aware of them at all. In simple terms, these were the secret papers and maps that held and captured the intrinsic detail and account of special trade voyages or at best guess held the details or volatile 'contents.'

If and when we begin searching such log books, we would soon discover that contained within the average log pages one would find a simple record of a ship's known inventory or cargo manifest, and was, in essence, a book that held the important locations of certain items on board the vessel that were stored in a specific order. Often, a handwritten note or two would be scribbled in the margins, or a sketch or picture would be inserted near the item list, and often supported by additional footnotes or inserts reporting the vessel's actual co-ordinates or highlighted key events that occurred on board the vessel in the form of a diary. Entries mostly comprising details of lands visited that contained valuable future inventory such as fruits, vegetables, flax, cocaine, coffee, linen, tea and perhaps gold, sapphire, diamonds, or even the odd holy artefact or items of commercial or intrinsic value and of great interest, which were all accounted for in fine detailed maritime specific terminology. But, most importantly, the log contained the last known location or whereabouts of a vessel whilst it was under sail. Albeit, we should still be cognizant that this log was no run of the mill account of a simple journey either, as average log books normally held details such as broken pieces of ships rigging, masts, damage, etc., or damaged cargo and on the very odd occasion in-house disputes between the crew. Anson's log, however, was not of that low level of account, and not by a long chalk, as this particular log book had actually belonged to the infamous and notorious Captain George Anson himself and that makes a huge difference for this narrative somewhat more interesting indeed. But let us first acknowledge that before George Anson got his grubby paws on this important deadly script, we must first acknowledge that some of the inserts, loose pages, and maps of various shape and dimension within this ledger had once been in the possession of several infamous sea-going naval characters and masters who once held deep knowledge of this deathly inventory and who would swear on pain of death that this parchment known as the 'Horseshoe Expedition ledger' never existed, or in the world of the Caribbean pirate life the 'The Ophir – Cara' exists and that was for good reason.

This important book and treasure map had originally belonged to a more infamous and colourful character in naval criminal history and that Pirate was one Edward Teach or (Thatch) aka Captain Blackbeard, who had a turbulent and fruitful adventure over two years as the most notorious pirate of them all. Albeit, he was also reported to have possessed a copy of the ancient Fernandez map document, and to his credit, he had been accountable for attacking almost forty- two ships whilst at sea including the Royal Navy, and may have had access to the detail and trade routes held within this deadly Horseshoe ledger. As Blackbeard deceived, lied, and slimed his way from meeting the gallows too early, he may have also struck a special trade deal or bargain with the Admiralty, claiming that he knew where the 'Incas' treasure trove actually was located and had dealt a deal with another infamous not so well known Marketeer called – **Captain George Anson,** who is the current owner. Anson was certainly an undisputed master mariner of the open seas and whilst acting as an ambassador to the British Admiralty, coupled with the British crown to be more exact, and may have had unlimited access to the highest authority in the land. But in reality, people like Sir Francis Bacon & George Anson were in part still pirates.

We should understand that Lord Anson was a man who was in simple terms much larger in life character as history would have us believe, and it was often said that one would hear the man before physically setting eyes upon his large and bulbous awkward frame, especially as he traversed or negotiated his way along the long open alleyways and corridors of the many state suites or offices within the offices of London's St James's buildings more often than not. Anson would often wander quite aimlessly at all times during the day in a state of mind that could only be described as being in a drunken stupor. But as a man, he was quite tolerable whilst in a private company as opposed to a state function where he may have tippled too much; additionally, it must be stated that on the odd occasion he was described as not of this earth during some public affairs of state. Although, this mode of arrogance was all occurring at a time in our history where pomp and circumstance ran rife and where this self-serving socialite buffoon would always try to be the centre of social attention, and this new societal model sadly fitted in very well with the arrogant 17th century elite landed gentry classes coupled with the tolerant ignorant society that fitted in very nicely for this era. But sadly, the master mariner was not known for his overwhelming prowess, charm, or uncanny wit either, nor for his ability to deal with normal people in a logical or respectful manner, or act in as much to say that he was likeable as far as close family was concerned. But on the whole, he was a somewhat aristocratic, self-serving, arrogant, un-charming, ignorant individual most of the time. The details recently disclosed in a London newspaper article where it was 'quoted' by an undisclosed source from the London press office stating that 'Anson being an embarrassment to the King's War Office.' But he was probably called far worse than that by most of his enemies or people who endured and suffered his ignorant attitude towards life in general and had done so on far too many an occasion.

The soft internal pages of the log book at first glance appeared to be made from a coloured pigment akin to an off white shade of colour almost bordering on a dull beige or dull yellow, but it was difficult to say for sure against the struggling candle light, and apart from a few bold type face letters in lower case that were dotted haphazardly across the page, it was a reasonable and very well presented piece of parchment. The overall layout of the writing block text and actual literal content of the layout was quite legible and had been laid out as if one was currently reading or scrutinising the ledger; it was almost as if the unknown reader had been searching for something in particular, or was updating or writing an entry and was certainly taking a lot of time to absorb its important content. Specifically as the juxta position of the quill pen and crucifix appeared to be denoting or was pointing to something extra special, but the question, for now, was: 'What was this special something?'

Was it a mystery treasure map or perhaps a secret rendezvous point in the Chilean archipelago, Peru, or nearer the Juan Fernandez islands? Or was it the Bahama islands? Or was there really a treasure trove hidden in the sand? Or was it another ledger highlighting a horde of conquistador booty containing barrels of silver coins? Or pieces of eight sitting under the sun or secluded in a church vault somewhere in Ethiopia or India perhaps? But sadly, at this juncture, Kemp Hastings could not tell exactly what any of it meant, but he was sure to find out soon enough. Therefore, apart from being a well-written log, it was still a run-of-the-mill **'list'** of activities executed from what would be deemed a chronicle of a ship's normal daily routines whilst at sea, or was it?

The detail simply held within this log – highlighted information that would allude to the current crew comprising of: (68) sixty-eight crew names and their respective duties, (12) twelve Officers including cadets or mid-shipmen, and a list of their assigned duties. But in essence, the ships complement or muster roll of staff which consisted mainly of low orders cooks, able-bodied sailors including the bosun and additional deck crew, alas, not forgetting the important trained naval gunners amongst several names of men joining and signing articles by signature or had signed on ships articles at the proverbial dotted line with their infamous 'X', and on the odd occasion a smudged thumbprint. The recorded information had been supported with dates and a few written side notes about the actual voyage itself, which was a normal practice with the added detail of which could only be described as quick scribblings in the left-hand margin. He noted a few words referring to The Conquistadors map, and although Hastings was a man not void of common logic, he had already heard of the 15th and 16th century raids across Peru and the pillaging of the Inca people, albeit he was more than aware that such golden trinkets included in the haul contained jewellery pieces that once belonged to the wife of Emperor Atahualpa, which had been taken in one of the many raids. And it is said that eight hundred so-called barrels of gold and silver coins had also been part of the grand loot. His thoughts remained in and around the tonnage that was reported in these acquisitions being an excess of six hundred tons carried on board many vessels.

Hastings was also cognisant that Anson had recently returned from one of his round the world journey's and had included, India, Madagascar, and Peru in his journals, although Hastings was more interested as to how many innocent sailors were being murdered or had suddenly and very conveniently died of cholera or scurvy to hide a great secret. And as we know that even the Scotsman Alexander Selkirk may have also been aware of the location as he himself had been left on an island to protect a great secret or perhaps was left just to die. Or was it a coincidence that after four years the man was eventually rescued by a recovery ship on an undisclosed expedition by British Naval forces who were also seeking a similar wealth of treasure that was known as the Horseshoe wealth and thought that he, Alexander Selkirk himself had somehow been part of the wider plot?

Hastings leaned forward and smoothed out the edges of the page with his right hand and folded the top right-hand corner down over itself; he did this in order to see more clearly the dull lettering which had been elegantly penned, although his efforts were futile as he could not see the lettering clearly due to the lighting in the dimly lit room. He then stopped struggling to concentrate his gaze in the darkness and searched the area and eventually found a small stub of candle wax sitting nearby and managed to shed some greater light on the page, and then as if by the magic of science, the cabin was now almost negotiable using the naked eye as the candle erupted into lighted splendour. Hastings for some reason slowly started biting at his top lip as he viewed and read the interesting pages and took precious time to contemplate the potential and valuable content of the account, reading each entry carefully and took extra time especially regarding detail about the whereabouts of some remote locations across the known globe.

Some of these locations included a potential pirate island stronghold called St Marie's isle, located off the coast of Madagascar, and additionally another small inlet known as Mahone Bay, near Nova Scotia, Canada (Arcadia), and Santa Clara Island near Chile. Then spied a small sketch of the country of Chile with the inscription 'D' and 'M' clearly marked at the entrance to what Hastings would say was a small inlet bay. He had also noticed that the letter '**D**' at the top of the page was written in bold Latin script and had been penned black ink with a thin red line struck through the middle of the arch of the lettering. The young naval officer continued to view each page very carefully then soon found the letter '**M**' and then began working very slowly and very deliberately identifying all the letters, and eventually found to his amazement that he had located a capital letter on every numbered page of the now very interesting log book. Each specific capital letter having been written in 'Latin script' and by all accounts, he had found the letters **D.M - O.U.O.S.V.A.V.V.**, which was an odd sort of anagram, and curiously, it had been written with clear deliberation and maturity in each of the page corners. The log would have typified George Anson's unique style and very personal way of recording daily maritime business on board the many vessels he had commanded, but in all his years, Hastings had never seen such a script so elegantly displayed, although he did smile when he noticed drawings on tiny horseshoes dotted on certain pages. And he knew that this particular log was a Royal Order, although in essence the book was very well maintained to reflect a certain level of naval administrative discipline in the style of clerical excellence and was still a fine example of careful maritime record keeping.

Captain Anson also knew that the ships log books were always looked after with great care and protection; however, the inserted pages or second log (hidden log) would never see the light of day and only viewed by the Captain's themselves or by senior Admiralty Officers in general or his peer group who simply demanded absolute Royal loyalty from within their ranks, and that meant details, details, details, because on the odd occasion it was not uncommon for a reigning 'Monarch' to request a viewing of a Frigate or merchant ship's voyage accounts. And the crown office often requested the official and legal log books to be presented at Royal court for scrutiny, which was often conducted under a process that served a great military purpose. Suffice to say that this parchment was very different one indeed from Anson's other most recent ship logs or from his prior merchant excursions and Kemp Hastings knew that for a fact. For some inexplicable reason, he also knew in his mind that this was an Admiralty cover up. Or why else would they have such a coding system on certain pages? The problem was that this code required a cipher code to decode the lettering, albeit it was obvious to him that it was a deception plan as he had witnessed the actual handover of the ship's log and charter boxes, which was also conducted under a blanket of secrecy when Anson had received the special boarding party prior to sailing into the waters of the Indian ocean.

As the First Officer of the vessel, even he himself had not been invited to attend the first meeting with the Admiralty visitors which sparked a certain air of distrust with him already as he was not part of the planned proceedings. It was either war records or it was a merchant deception plan, and he understood very well that the log book was going to be the '**key**' and would be acting as a double-entry book, therefore, disguising the actual or real intent of the 'orders' to be executed. Hastings as First Officer and a few select Knights of the Templar Order had already joined the crew of the new vessel under the guise of general seaman, but in reality, they were on a special mission to source and locate some Holy relics that had gone missing due to high seas piracy earlier and that two vessels carrying the Holy Orders inventory had been recently ransacked, and somewhere along the line, Solomon's treasure had suddenly become very vulnerable.

Hastings and the team had embarked on a crusade that would eventually bring droves upon droves of treasure seekers in their wake consisting of dreamers, sailors, scientists, rogues, vagabonds, and the worst kind of all the upper-class buffoons who were already rich enough to live in abject splendour but wanted to prove to daddy that they were made of the real stuff in order to claim their eternal inheritance. And, in some cases, it was take this opportunity or be forced to join and serve the Military and die in horrendous battles like great uncle Albert did, and, as an example, he died so well. Uncle Albert died an officer who was skewered by a bayonet in some obscure country or other and was run through by a native and got a medal for all his troubles and efforts. But in stark contrast to the normal working peasant, these were all the people who sought fame and fortune for one reason or another and wanted to walk in the footsteps of ancient glory hunting heroes and social giants which often led these discoverers into the very dangerous footsteps of history. As we tread carefully through the veiled shadows of time, we will identify a trait that will run rife up through the centuries to follow as the many would-be **treasure-seekers** of modern-day search tirelessly for the riches that were to be had, but that is of course should they ever decipher the many secret codes along the way and of course the famous Shugborough or DM Code in its entirety first.

O.U.O.S.V.A.V.V
D M

CHAPTER THREE

'Kemp Hastings'

Gentlemen Officer Lieutenant Kemp Hastings R.L. (Royal Lodge) stood tall at five foot nine in his stocking soles and weighs in at eighty-eight kilos and was of a fair athletic build. His fine chiselled jawline and piercing blue eyes coupled with a crop of soft light brown hair made this young man of a mere forty-four years old a very good catch for any young maiden wishing to hook up and embark on a journey of an intrepid lifestyle, an existence that would be interesting, especially whilst investigating life at sea beyond the Admiralty. Nevertheless, Hastings was clean-cut and very self–aware. Academics would say that people who know and understood that their emotional intelligence levels are very astute may be quite quick to anticipate who would make enemies and who make friends. Hastings was indeed such a man that desired wealth and recognition for his many efforts and exploits, especially as he stood very silent for approximately one full minute gazing over the interesting parchment page that sat open before him (and he was making enemies rapidly).

In his mind's eye, he knew that the ancient Roman lettering dotted across the page meant something very important indeed and there was another language to consider; was it Spanish or Greek and how important was it? He had no inclination and had very little idea of what it really was that he was looking at or what it all really meant as yet, but in his mind's eye, he knew that he for one was sure hell-bent on finding out why the log was so neatly preserved by Anson because, quite simply, this notation was conducted by a notorious sea Captain very deliberately and he was a man who would never in a million years have taken so much time and deliberation or care whilst paying so much attention to detail as so to scribe the entries so elegantly in this special hidden message. And George Anson would never in his own lifetime waste precious time in doing so without a very good reason indeed, unless, of course, it was a highly important one.

This Captain had taken so much care to place the arrangement of letters exactly on a numbered line of the pages specifically and he had done so in such a way that he had systematically worked across each page in the log with great care and precision as would a scientist or surgeon conducting an important medical operation or experiment. And that fact alone meant that the secret hidden within these pages was deemed life-threatening for him not to do so. Captain George Anson was not a man who did things by half measure or would simply play off the cuff or haphazardly take a chance and dive headlong into any issue of which he had not already calculated the risk as to why he should do so in the first place; Anson was an exacting person in his decision making and was impeccable to the point of utter annoyance, therefore, being habitually precise in his manner. He was a master mariner possessing the quality and unique leadership skills and experience which were never really brought into question by the Admiralty, but in his tenure, he had experienced deaths on his vessels either due to cholera, scurvy, or malnutrition. Although in the era of sail, this was quite a global problem, and Captains were protected by statute law because such ailments could manifest themselves under many conditions beyond the control of the skipper or doctor and we will soon discover that his Captaincy and authority were well earned, along with his naval achievements, which are very clearly recorded in British maritime historical records.

However, whilst socialising in the public domain, Anson was someone else entirely. He was always seen to be unwavering in his arrogance as a man and could be deemed at times an ignorant swine and very cold and heartless person especially when dealing with affairs of good or even bad seamanship as he dished out his discipline, or more so, when dealing with matters that concerned the hidden order of the Knights Templar or where the Priory of Sion that was setting out their stall regarding their very secret desires.

But, Lieutenant Kemp Hastings on the other hand was another kettle of fish entirely and he also knew and understood only too well that if he was caught removing the official log book from the Royal Naval vessel itself, then he was in deep trouble. He also understood that he would certainly face the Admiralty and incur their unreserved wrath and that he would be severely reprimanded and possibly endure a punishment that would involve unleashing the proverbial cat of nine tails to come out and play, and thus, being whipped to within an inch of his very life. But for this man, this cruel torture was not on the cards, but he still knew that he had to be careful and act over cautiously if he was to survive the next few hours. Albeit, his current quest was one of the utmost importance and the cat of nine tails would be the least of his worries should the 'Black Lodge' manage to steal the important Ship's ledger before the officer got his hands on it.

The Black Lodge was quite obscure as to who they really were. Rumours were that they were the British-backed masons but Hastings had heard rumours that they were a secret clan chasing the conquistadors for the island map of Juan Fernandez. Juan Fernandez himself was an explorer charged with securing and hiding riches beyond the imagination and the 'map' was the key and the 'archer' the star sign was the indicator, hence, why the Black Lodge who had knowledge of this map were unrelenting in their search for the cartograph and didn't care who they would have to kill in order to achieve it. Hastings, with only a few minutes or so to spare, had already viewed the contents of the secret ledger and had begun quizzing the newly opened page slowly but surely and traced the folds on the paper with his left index finger by running his digit along the leading edges of the first and second page borders, only stopping at each corner of the page to view the printing and acknowledge the cypher code. He then refolded the second page across the first page to see what he could make of the geometry and styling of the print in question. The page had been folded over several times and he began smoothing over the edges and ridges that had been deliberately formed into a shape on the opposite page. At first, the image looked like a half diamond symbol, or a zodiac sign, then it could have been half a naval compass rose or a northern star figure, but he knew eventually the page would reveal its true secret if folded correctly, and perhaps it was just a symbol, one of which would signify the other half of the star of David (Jerusalem) or display lines of a topographic navigational compass rose, an indicator maybe, leading him or the reader to a big 'x' which was marking the spot, or lead him to a place where great riches lay ready for plundering.

Hastings had no trouble deciphering some parts of the Latin symbols and he knew and understood enough about naval map reading to read the compass rose with great competence as every naval officer of the day should. But now all that the incumbent Officer of the watch had to do was simply locate the other half of the interesting cipher code or at least find the actual compass rose headings or identify the start point on the drawing. Deep down in his gut, he knew that there would be some references somewhere on the pages and he intended to find them and put them all together, but still he reserved a notion in his head that another answer or a clue may still well be lurking somewhere nearby in the cabin and it was most likely to be very obvious. The ledger was too easy to be translated and he knew the incumbent Captain was not that stupid or dumb enough to be so predictable, and yet, for some odd reason, he still had an inclination that another part of this conundrum could be sitting in blind obscurity and could be simply perched not too far away from his vision or the real answer could even be as close as sitting on the chart table at the aft end of the wardroom. He muttered to himself, 'C'mon, Anson, give it to me. Where is the bloody cipher key? Where is the notebook?' Whispering softly again to himself, he then picked up a single small map that depicted the continent of Africa and read the words as they appeared. 'Ophir, et Ethiopia'. The words had been scribbled across the top edge of the page.

Then, there it was again, the word 'archer' 'D' only written this time in very light pencil near a small sketch of the star constellation 'The Archer or Sagitarius', then the words 'Pinaki Trinity-Scorpius' in bold lettering with the star sign elegantly drawn. Hastings waited a few moments longer and contemplated his actions before closing the log and began stuffing all the vellum pages into his Royal Navy Officers tunic whilst simultaneously planning his imminent escape from the frigate. He started to scan the immediate area feeling somewhat like a human travelling library having borrowed a few other documents for the longer-term during his visit into the private quarters of the Captain. He stopped abruptly. Had he heard footsteps or was it the ship's real cat chasing its own tail again? Or was it just his imagination? And then by instinct, he held his breath, turned half left, and proceeded directly towards the chart room watching and listening as he made his way through the long corridor intending to quiz the chart table to check out the current sea chart, as Anson would often scribble down the odd number or the name of something he was thinking about and would write a word or two near the map's legend to remind him.

It was one of those Hastings inclinations again; it was a moment of simply 'act quickly - worry later.'

As he moved through the vessel with stealth, he glanced into the wardroom and entered just for a few moments instantly quizzing the writing desk and then began slowly gazing over its red leather-clad top, observing only a few folded maps and some inventory parchments sitting off to the left of the 'live' chart table. But there was nothing that stuck out from the ordinary or anything that would raise any suspicions regarding the use of symbols, but sadly, the chart was clean. Having made his way back into the Captain's domain, he spied an older sea chest sitting in the far corner of the bunk and half-hidden by a Naval Officers' jacket that had been draped over to one side of the chest. In the 16th and 17th centuries, it was not uncommon for officers to have two or even three sea chests in their quarters or offices whilst they were at sea, although this particular sea chest had a very serious looking locking mechanism indeed, and yet when he leaned over it and simply flicked open its heavy lid with apparent ease, he started thinking: why leave it open? Why? Was the heavy chest not locked like normal, and then on the spur of the moment, the officer unceremoniously delved straight into the abyss of almost nothingness of any importance, only soon to discover just a few shirts, two pairs of pantaloons, a leather belt, and some more paperwork hidden within the chest? As he continued to fumble around a bit longer, he soon realised that there was what appeared to be a loose panel of wood or a false bottom within the trunk. He recalled thinking again that surely this Captain was not so stupid or even negligent enough in his manner as to leave the tell tail thin red cord deliberately exposed for all and sundry to see, unless, of course, Anson had planned it that way for him; the box itself was simply left unlocked.

Timing was important and Hastings had tried to time things nicely it was now nearing zero five twelve in the morning and the vessel was reasonably quiet. He paused then pulled out a small red leather carry case from within the confines of the casket; it was just then that he heard the heavy footsteps of someone approaching the wardroom from along the port side corridor. He stopped what he was doing and began spying out between the thin gap between the cabin door itself and the heavy oak frame, but he could still see nothing. Holding his breath for a few seconds longer, he listened just in case the crew members had super-sensitive hearing and could hear him swallowing and gulping or even gasping for air as they stood nearby. From what he could deduce, it sounded more like two persons had entered the lower corridor and from the sound of the shuffling feet across the creaky wooden deck boards, they were nearer the forward end as opposed to midships, and, of course, he recognised the distinct noise of heavy leather scraping across the loose planks nearer the ward room.

He knew most of the sounds that creaked and squeaked around the vessel as all ships had their signature or idiosyncratic noises of which possessed their own melody of movement, although he could not be one hundred percent sure and, therefore, thought that he would probably be outnumbered should a healthy man to man fist fight erupt. Stuffing the documents deeper into the back of his breeches, he tightened his belt and straightened himself upright. Taking no time at all, he closed the door softly and slid the locking mechanism into place thinking that the oak sea chest was rather empty apart from a small set of handwritten notes which he had grabbed and stuffed into his inner jacket pocket, still thinking and wondering that he had watched Anson time after time stuff a vast range of bits and bobs into its fair-sized innards of the box over several months, including the Ships Log carry case, and yet he was still amused and slightly disappointed at the same time that the kiste was almost empty of any real booty. Although, for the now, Hastings thought he had acquired sufficient information for him to carry out his ongoing quest.

CHAPTER FOUR

'Visitors'

On the upper deck of the HMS Wager, three figures had stepped on to the gangway and were making their way on board the vessel to seek an audience with Captain Cheap and Captain Anson. The Bosun was first to stop the visitors with pistols at the ready and waited to interrogate the men and was quite anxious to ask them as to their intentions of arriving so early in the morning at the vessel. Especially as the vessel had landed only a couple of weeks or so ago at the merchant trading port Antofagasta in Chile. The taller of the visitors were first to talk and stepped onto the wobbly gangway first and confronted the Bosun. 'Good morning that man, I am Lieutenant Freeman of his 'His Majesty's Naval Council and these are my dedicated councillors, Lieutenant Hardy and Lieutenant Willis, and we are here to have a meeting with your Captain.' The Bosun acknowledged the visitors and tipped his hat forward as a sign of acknowledgement as he spied the Officer of the Watch walking towards them. Then he spoke: 'One moment, gentlemen, I will inform the deck Officer.' The Bosun then approached the oncoming officer and stated that Lieutenants Freeman, Hardy, and Willis had stepped on board supporting their new Admiralty leather footwear and Uniform carrying orders from the state and sought an audience to converse with the Captain. After their short conversation was had between the Officer of the watch and the Bosun, the men were deemed of good intent and were to be escorted below decks by Gary Bertie - Bosun extraordinaire who accompanied the un-announced visitors below decks. Unknown to Captain Cheap or Captain Anson at this time, both the incumbent skippers were about to suffer a very rude professional awakening and would be exposed to certain mutiny from their renegading crews after the Admiralty staff had left the vessel of course. It is with hindsight that George Anson would have to account not only for his own actions that day, but probably those of Captain Cheap as well who had recently been plagued with illness. And the good Captain Anson in the kindness of heart had stepped into the breach to take control of things. Albeit today or at any time was not going to be a good day to be Captain Anson, especially regarding His Majesty's visitors as the on-duty Captain. But in reality, Anson was currently somewhat indisposed, well not totally indisposed, but to put things in another way whilst placing things in finer point detail on the subject, the Captain lay unconscious on the wooden deck having been exposed to a rather swift violent encounter and a heavy blow to the back of his skull from a rather large heavy brass British naval spyglass telescope. The instrument, of course, was complete with purser's mark and signs of fair age. The obvious instrument with its unique size and shape being tubular and quite robust would easily be recognised as the long-distance state of the art spy-glass, albeit obviously this particular telescope had an additional function and was not just a mere telescope but was indeed a fine, robust, and most suitable instrument for rendering someone unconscious, and of which had just become an excellent example of a 'Kosh' for this exact purpose. This practical use of such a technical instrument was perhaps not so much a well-known fact of practical employment and certainly is not mentioned in the end user's guide or seaman's handbook at this time.

On hearing the commotion from the upper deck of the vessel, Hastings instantly froze and stood bolt upright then tipping his hat whilst apologising to the Skipper for his unprecedented attack as he stepped over the bulbous torso of the unconscious captain. Although Anson remained inert and was quite dead to the world and was quite oblivious to the unfolding events above decks. On the other hand, good old Captain Charlie Cheap was in a state of induced slumber brought on by consuming an unhealthy amount of leaves and mushrooms prescribed by the ship's surgeon and cook coupled with a few yard arms of alcohol donated by Mister Pusser the Rum merchant. Kemp Hastings, the now would-be thief and human library, waited to hear what the two men in the wardroom were up to and had guessed that they had gone back towards the galley. He then waited a few more seconds and took a very deep breath and stealthily exited the room, almost tiptoeing across the inner decks whilst still attempting to hold his breath. The wardroom and the Captain's bunk were co-located on the quarterdeck and the main exit door led directly into the path of potential oncoming visitors if they had entered through the port side alleyway. In anticipation of encountering any of the crew, Hastings had already pulled open a small exit flap that had been constructed into the wooden bulkhead and had exited the space via what would be deemed as the Bosun's 'smuggling bolt hole', which was, in essence, a man-sized makeshift emergency escape hatch or window designed for such occasions. As the young man exited the vessel and slowly climbed down the makeshift rope, his hands soon became skin ripped and very sore and warm from the friction against the rope and increased in pain as the entwined hemp created more heat as it cut deep into the sailor's hands, and more so painful as the salt sodden twain bit deeper into his soft skin. Sadly, these were the hands of a knowledgeable and academic man and not the veteran hands of a rough and well-seasoned seafarer or Bosun, albeit both his hands hurt and burned like hell. The now very ex-naval officer then dropped the last few feet straight into the waiting wooden dinghy below and had managed to remain unnoticed by the crew above who were busy loading stores shore side. Hastings the newly adopted pirate and maritime documents thief slowly began rowing his way towards the outer harbour wall in order to escape any unwanted detection and simply acted very carefully as not to be seen by any of the vessel crew. A few minutes later, the alert was raised and the ship's full complement were now busy searching across the nooks and crannies of the vessel and running across the decks like headless chickens as various bells and whistles were being blown and peeled out loud enough to wake up the proverbial dead. They were now summoning all the ship's crew to muster on the upper decks.

Hastings had stopped rowing and watched eagerly as Anson appeared at the lower deck cabin window on the aft deck and swung the heavy wooden framed window open in a fit of rage. Hastings stopped everything and picked up the spyglass and spied from a distance the angered face of the Captain as he stared directly back at him whilst still busy scratching the back of his head. At the same time, Hastings noticed that the skipper was clenching his fist perhaps whilst holding a small book or letter? The new age Pirate Mr. K Hastings esquire could not tell exactly what other item he was holding was as he himself was too far away and had blended in with other Antafagosta harbour life. Luckily for him, the dockyard morning activity awoke within its somewhat dark buildings and unwelcoming walls where the local inhabitants had come to life amongst the suburban squalor, and judging by the sight of the nearby prison building as the windows began opening and the unpleasant flush of human effluent was being poured indiscriminantly into the off white brown foamy waters below was perhaps not the best sort of thing to witness first thing at a new dawn.

The visiting officers meanwhile had started to descend the corridors of the vessel and were making enough noise to wake up the proverbial dead, and had just found Captain Anson wandering in the corridor like a lost soul in a confused stupor still holding his right hand over the back of his head and yet still carried a small booklet in his left hand when he suddenly started spouting a hail of orders, 'Bosun, Bosun!' He squealed shouting at the top of his voice for the Bosun to appear, but after the fourth attempt at summoning the man, it was reported that he had gone missing and was nowhere to be found.

The visiting officers took the time to enter the ward room and waited patiently to meet with Captain Anson. The taller of the visitors Lieutenant Freeman tended to the skipper and had sat the Captain down whilst attempting to subdue the patient and gave the Captain a cloth bathed in water to nurse his swollen head. He then asked the dumbest of questions, 'What happened, sir, if we had known you had problems we would have.' Anson interjected abruptly, 'You would have done what exactly, mister whatever your name is, as you were above decks, man; and besides there was nothing you could have done anyway. I was struck from behind as I picked up my ale and my log book.' Anson flinched then jumped up shouting, 'Oh! No! The log book where is the ships log book; someone has stolen it along with my papers.' Anson was very agitated and started gripping his hands together. 'Gentlemen, we have a huge problem if you will go out on to the decks, flood the streets with the crew if necessary, and go find my log book. You can't miss it; it is large and very distinctive, and find the bloody Bosun and the First Officer Mister Hastings. And someone please get Captain Cheap on to his feet.' For the next half an hour, the vessel went into lock down and search mode as the crew had already scrambled onto the streets to find the Bosun, Hastings, and the important log book. Meanwhile, Anson, whilst still nursing a sore head, stood up and gazed out of the open window out into the wide dockyard. Hastings was still hiding in the shadows under the jail building, having heard the pandemonium that had erupted across the vessel and was ironically hiding the small craft out of view, which was casting a darker shadow over the lighter backdrop of the rustic and well used wooden jetty, having just managed to tuck the boat under the large wooden platform near the building complex and was luckily out of sight. Hastings had caught a glimpse of the blue jacket of the Bosun and his colleagues as they darted off the gangway and into the nearby dark alleyway and knew that they should be making their arduous way to the agreed rendezvous point in the next few hours.

Kemp Hastings had originally started a very promising career in the British Navy and was elevated to the rank of warranted Gunner very quickly. Then he had a stint as midshipman for only two years as he had an earlier merchant shipping background moved upwards to Purser, which by some accounts was not 'in line with naval conformity as far as a naval career was concerned', but for now, he was the captain of a small wooden rowing boat and rowed in fear of his life or at least driven by the fear of being caught and with a solid Naval career in the age of the sail sitting firmly behind him; he smiled somewhat arrogantly, very much content in his thinking that this line of action or excitement was far more fun and definitely more exciting than being one of a commissioned officer in the King's failing navy without any real authority. But, in real terms, he would have gone far up the ranks to at least to the dizzy heights of Commander or even Captain, but for Hastings, this was not to be the case as far as he was concerned. What he wanted was a quick buck and an easy way of life from now on. His other duty or impending crusade, however, was of course for the holy order and it was nothing more and nothing less. His life really depended upon the outcome and it appeared to him that his new partner in crime was also going to be a certain challenge as he was a well-known Officer called William Kidd currently employed by the East India Trading Company, and had somehow emerged into his life as an unintroduced partner. It was from this onset that it was to become an odd kind of relationship and one of which that had been arranged more through serendipity than by anything else. But each man comprehending and knowing that Captain Anson had definitely lost his way in the grander scheme of things and wanted nothing but wealth and power, which left the man in a place never to be trusted ever again, especially now as they both had donned the mantle of protection of the order's hidden wealth—whatever that actually was or meant. But according to them both, they were 'duty bound' to humanity to deliver on a deal neither of them could negotiate their way out of. Kidd was a fairly well-to-do man, but he never seemed to have taken leave of his origins as a Dundee sailor and always yearned to return to the Scottish city and make good his life. But the deal with the order was a psychological contract between the Holy Order of the Knights of Santiago and Malta and the two seafarers than that of the Navy and were secretly recruited but remained unaware of one another's real background. Thus, somewhere, somehow, the powers that be had brought them together under the most strangest of circumstances as the merchant shipping world was being hurled into turmoil and the Knights Templars had engaged these two men who were British mariners at heart and who were not only in the 'know' as to how pirates and the maritime world operate but were both quite devious in their own right as sea-rovers, thus, were recruited directly to serve the Order.

But, sadly for Captain Anson, who now nurses a very sore head along with his declining relationship with the Templar Order, which was subsiding rapidly as the London Society of Masons had now no real direct course of action to take, and could only standby and make excuses for their confusion. And the Order and Anson's relationship was now in suspension as the Knights had serious reservations about Anson's motives, especially as the incumbent Captain had displayed traits of piracy himself and who had been working under strict instructions from the London based Naval institution and the crown, which, in essence, meant bring wealth to the nation at all costs, and greed was becoming the order of the day. The same deal that was offered to Captain William Kidd a couple of years earlier and the 'command' was: 'rape and pillage the high seas for wealth', but Kidd had other ideas. However, The Holy Order did not share this common value and that meant innocent people would suffer at yet another pirating nation that would have to be tamed. Although it could be stated that Captain Kidd had become a more irate sort of pirate than most of his contemporaries and his enemies were, but in reality, Kidd was dependable as far as the Order was concerned, although he would often demonstrate great empathy as the real man whilst displaying signs of affection and care when it came to certain people in his life, and we should add that not a great deal was known of his family apart from his marriage to Sarah Bradley Cox Oort in 1691. And William Kidd had kept it that way by design to secure their future safety.

Kidd was a simple but greedy business person and was a man driven by the notion of wealth and power to the point of obsession, but he had been tamed by his drive to appease the lord above and the Order, but George Anson on the other hand had clearly overstepped the boundary of common decency driven by the same desire for wealth completely, and his future legacy would be driven by his veracity for riches and power. In his tenure at sea, George Anson had stood by and watched many men die under his direct command from such horrible things like bouts of scurvy brought on by the lack of fresh fruit that would have contained simple vitamin 'c' for his crew, or had endured bouts of Cholera coupled with the suffering long term malnutrition which had manifested itself on so many journeys across the open seas, perhaps due to the lack of careful planning or simply not purchasing sufficient stores to survive the long journey ahead in the first place. Also, very much according to Captain William Kidd, George Anson was no angel and no better a sea Captain than the average land lubber murderer, whoever jumped a naval ship and took command.

Kidd would never compare himself to be on par with the man, but the arrogance and ignorance of George Anson adorned with a certain amount of wealth, which had already been acquired by his family and of which had made Anson very intolerable in the eyes of his peers and men. Although it seemed plausible to them 'sort' of people to have their own aims and goals in life mostly achieved at the cost and suffering of everyone else below them. And that ignorance alone was making life hell for all British mariners and old sea dogs that sail the proverbial seven seas, some of which chose that way of life deliberately in order not to conform or obey any arrogant or bigoted Naval dominance but chose instead to chase the Buccaneer way and code of life operating as free spirits and, of course, with no ethics being firmly applied. Kidd was the instrument that permitted both of these traits to run free amongst his crews to a certain degree.

CHAPTER FIVE

'DM Code'

The Adventure Galley

The DM code may well be a series of ten cipher symbols in the form of alphabet letters that could hold the secret as to where the treasures of the infamous Knights Templar may actually be located. The actual DM Code itself can be deciphered in one way, therefore, if we acknowledge the current alphabet below and relate each number to a corresponding letter where we can soon deduce that basic codes and hidden secrets of locations can be broken down to meet certain frameworks or languages. But in order to stimulate the brain cells and urge the intellectual juices to flow a little more within the minds of readers of this narrative, both Kemp Hastings and William Kidd would probably have liked you to consider the following approach to a very simple code-breaking exercise whilst taking part in a maritime navigational conundrum. Kemp Hastings sat in front of the Captain and they both reviewed the following details with the greatest of interest. Hastings had placed his index finger in the middle of the vellum plan and continued with his recital. 'Well, Captain, for starters, let us not get hung up on hearsay and rumours as they never turn out to be what you think they are and that's why I wanted to have this 'tet a tet' face to face with you so that we can both be on the same course as it were. For our first attempt at this code-breaking 'shennigans', we should keep in mind that George Anson is indeed a Master Mariner and a master seafarer, which may trigger the necessity to adopt a certain maritime mindset whilst we are referring to naval marine topography, and to think about marine mapping as a priority in order to break this very simple code, a secret that Anson may or may not have put together. Therefore, opposed to what we know about land type maps or cartographs.' Kidd nodded his head and agreed as if he was actually interested as Hastings rambled on. 'In simple terms, let us use the main letters of the British alphabet that can correspond to a sequential number in turn. A=1, B=2, C=3, etc… You get the idea. Now in the main, that would be the logical thing to do, but herein lies a serious problem and there may be a slight hiccup with this approach, especially as the numbering might have to be shuffled to makes more sense, or if we were going to be using the infamous **Fibonacci code** sequence as is commonplace in some very secret societies so I hear. Then the code once deciphered as stated above would not make any sense at all as the letters would not match the numbers.

- *The Fibonacci Sequence is the series of numbers: 0, 1, 1, 2, 3, 5, 8, 13, 21, 34, … The next number is found by adding up the two numbers before it.*

Therefore, using the simple alphabet as I think Anson may have done, an example being that the A=1 approach can decipher all ten (10) letters of the DM code in a row and we should have in essence a ten-figure **map or grid reference**, but if you see the Ships log pages here on the highlighted pages.' Hastings pointed to each of the letters and numbers on the pages then continued: 'We can see that Anson had clearly written these capital letters on each page and this is where I think the page numbers are the actual keys, but they do not make up any map references that's for sure. What do you think?' Kidd openly agreed and nodded his head again and let his imagination and intellect dwell for a bit in order to fathom how simple this code-breaking stuff really is, or conversely how very difficult it can become.

Kidd was already considering the many variables that may have to be considered but sadly it has taken over two hundred and fifty years to date in order to reach this particular point in code-breaking, and the author of the ledger provides you with a stark warning and that caveat is not to embark on some half-baked treasure-seeking crusade without firstly reviewing all the potential risks to life and limb or even dare to venture out into adventure land ill-prepared for a journey of discovery whilst searching for such fantastic mystical treasures. Hastings continued with his recital and session on code-breaking Pirate style. 'Therefore, Captain, here is a table of what I have come up with using the simple alphabet method. Now, all we have to do is plot a course.' Kidd smiled. 'Not so fast, Mister Hastings. This is not that easy.'

A	B	C	D	E	F	G	H	I	J	K	L	M	N	O	P	Q	R	S	T	U	V	W	X	Y	Z
1	2	3	4	5	6	7	8	9	10	11	12	13	14	15	16	17	18	19	20	21	22	23	24	25	26
D.O.U.O.S.V.A.V.V.M																									
5	15	20	15	18	21	1	21	21	13																

- *Eastings 51 520 15 18 deg Northings 21 2113deg*

- *Northings 51 520 15 18 deg Eastings 211 21 21 13 deg*

Hastings then read out the numbers of the corresponding lines and pages again taken from Anson's ships log, starting with the first page he had encountered.

- 'Pages- 6,16,16,33, 49, 90,94,96,33,0'

Then scribbled the lettering in the order they had actually been removed from the log book of the HMS Wager.

- 16 90 94 16 6 - 49 90 96 33 0

- D O U S V - V A V M

Kidd then read the numbers that were written down as he listened to Hastings and could see no process as to why the numbers would make any sense at all less for the obvious reference to a specific line in the log book or a page; he then ran his finger over the numbers again and made a mental note, 06161633 4990909496, then all of a sudden and he smiled a big broad grin then said a few choice words, 'Tell me, why are the numbers not in numerical sequential order?' He asked whilst observing that the pages were not logical. Hastings acknowledged. 'Well only half the letters were written in the Ships master Log and the other letters were written in the **unofficial log**, so I had to decide which ones were in sequence; it made sense to take page one from each log.' Kidd then interrupted, 'Okay, given that logical approach then you may just have something interesting. I would say 'Madagascar'. These are just simple co-ordinates of the island; they are the map references with the Northings and Eastings for the island of Madagascar, my dear fellow. This is a map reference to the East side of the island by the way and this was probably where Anson was most likely heading when he wrote the notes in the HMS Wager's log book. But have you considered just starting from number one at 'zed' as is number 26, then you also soon discover that you have lost 6 to 1 as numbers, then it gets interesting? DM – 13' 0, that could be degrees or it could be in nautical miles.'

Z	Y	X	W	V	U	T	S	R	Q	P	O	N	M	L	K	J	I	H	G	-	F	E	D	C	B	A
26	25	24	23	22	21	20	19	18	17	16	15	14	**13**	12	11	10	09	08	07	-	0	0	0	0	0	0

But I would guess that Anson would have planned the rendezvous location in advance as to where the British Navy was going to hold up their fleet whilst planning for their reprisal attacks on the renegade pirates that sail these coast lines. I had heard that the British East India Company had engaged some influential partners, including British Royalty, as they want us one hundred percent out of the equation. I would bet this is where they planned to meet up before attacking the ships of the Dutch, French, and Pirate communities in one strike. However, Mister Hastings, that aside, but do you know there is also a darker secret when it comes to these types of codes? Have you ever heard of the Priory code? I can see your logic is quite plain to the common eye, but remember as you say there are codes that can be used to mark locations and you, my dear chap, may not be aware of what is called the Priory code. And it does not start with number one (1) either, it starts with number (9). There are other numbers to consider also like number (22) for example, but we would have to spend a lot of time deciphering this part.'

Hastings leant back into the wooden chair and thought for a few moments and was compelled to agree with Kidd at this point. 'I think that's what actually could happen if the British head off and hide out of sight for a few weeks, then probably wait to hear news of vessels coming onto the islands, and then they would attack. You know Hastings, the St Mary's Isle, is a lovely place. I have been there many times but Madagascar itself is too unruly for me. I want to live on Saint Mary's Isle and live to a ripe old age with chickens, pigs beer, and a shed load of gold.' Kidd smiled an awkward sort of smile then spoke, 'I have my life sorted on that blessed isle and I do have much to do to for getting things nice and settled. Do you know I also have a home in New York? It is a nice, big townhouse and was a good price too. And I will certainly have to visit there at some point as I have things to take care of and people to protect, and my thoughts are plenty, but I will tell you that I have a great secret that concerns the Isle of Saint Mary's and that secret Mister Hastings is why I have a house located there on the island with a wee gold mine and a drinking bar 'one-eyed jacks' and a lovely lady who takes care of me.' Hastings smiled and responded, 'C'mon, skipper, we can all go to Madagascar and dance on the islands and have many ladies to take care of us, skipper. Even an old goat like you could have fun in Madagascar.' Kidd shuffled awkwardly. 'Well, Mister Hastings, that may be so, but I have and I still do have things to do, but promise me one thing, though, the next time you visit St Mary's, go find my watering hole named 'one eyed jacks' and say hello to a girl called Willemina. And if you ever need any help from her, tell her that her feet are blessed and Kidd sent you, she will then know that I have sent you. Anyways, more important things; I recall hearing about this General Juan Fernandez and this exciting Treasure Map. Mind you, that was long ago, although it was said to have had special keys or indicators with numbers and letters scribbled all over the vellum to help in deciphering the code, but sadly, no one could make sense of it all. And that, my friend, was why the Admiralty had sent our industrious 'Anson' and the HMS Wager on his early global travels in the first place. This expedition was simply an Admiralty deception ploy. It was a con to use British funding to go find the treasure of the Incas, which could have been the same booty as the Treasure of Solomon. And be aware, Mister Hastings, in the next week or so, we are going to meet some very dangerous and ruthless characters and we had better be ready because that concerns these special maps and charts.'

CHAPTER SIX

'The Literal Context: The Arcadian Shepherd'

The Arcadian shepherds ciphertexts demonstrate that there are literally thousands of ways to decipher and interpret or misinterpret the actual DM code and each code may well sit in the correct parish and could answer the inquisitor for their unique and very personal purpose of discovery. But we should also note that the aligned eight letters could simply be a coded dedication to George Anson's deceased spouse. This is perhaps a love note and simply being written in Latin 'acronym' for the use of the Latin phrase – Optimae Uxoris Optimae Sororis Viduus Avantissmus, Vovit Virtubis, or 'Best of Wives Best of Sisters, to your Virtues.' Hastings smiled again before talking, 'The final message from a most devoted widower perhaps, or maybe a clue which is an enshrouded message into something far more important.' He stopped his recital whilst staring directly back at Kidd, then he stated that this may well be one of many such Latin translations attributed to the actual DM code itself, but as far as Kemp Hastings and William Kidd were concerned, this was just after a thought that was to be discussed later and dismissed as a fanciful notion based on an old oil painting painted by Nicolas Poussin back in the day. And that was many years before being etched as a Bas-Relief into stone resulting in a very sinister deadly game of cat and mouse with some serious institutions for the future. A game played by some rather nasty people and politicians across the elite gentry and it was a game that prompted many seafarers to take flight and who as individuals had circumnavigated the high seas in their quest to acquire vast riches whilst often sailing under horrendous weather conditions such as hurricanes, Tornado, and Tsunami, and some of them had survived the deadly storms to reach their life long goals.

These treasure seekers inspired by the DM Code had sailed off in their droves to obscure locations dotted across the known globe, which is where we would find that each treasure seeker was simply living out a dream in order to search the ocean waves for the potential of discovering great treasures. And sadly, many never returned to their homeland and loved ones, and if and when they returned they very disappointed men and women. We would find somewhere amongst the many records of the East India Company as an example, who hold many informative records in their extensive library and would keep safe the merchant shipping details regarding ships that had been lost at sea without any suitable explanation or no records. However, as an organisation, they had at least in their tenure took time to maintain a comprehensive record as best they could, and on occasions, they released extracts of their accounts periodically whilst accounting for the merchant ships that were attacked throughout the colonies by The French, The Dutch, The Arabs and the British, where each vessel was recorded as having been pillaged of their cargo and the crew left to survive or die and often left without rations or fresh water, which ultimately led to many deaths.

In the height of the high seas piracy realm, many ships were simply being deliberately run aground by their own Captains whilst evading attack by pirates or were simply forced to breach the coast line as they were being chased by looters and pirates whose only intention was to simply pillage and murder. And we should, therefore, remember that this Buccaneer life was a life at sea fantasy and adventure written and captured by many great authors who idolised many unruly Pirates and characters by choice. We should however never dismiss the real fact that some of these Pirates were nasty, horrible people and indeed scallywags who had murdered many innocent people in their tenure as sea terrorists or were certainly complicit in the demise of local villages, companies, and communities that had set up their homestead or businesses on the mainland of India, Chile, Malaysia or on the islands around Madagascar that were attacked frequently by these pirates.

We understand this because it has been very well documented in historical records that several great men and women had perished in their pursuits of their own desires, but sadly, for those poor, unfortunate souls, it is in stark reality that their lives perished quickly either only to be claimed by Davy Jones himself or were caught in the clutches of the dangerous oceans or their horrific enemies. Although as far as the **DM** conundrum is concerned, one would guess that George Anson may have actually played a major role also in this massive deception planning and was perhaps most likely to be an instrument of strategy leading up to and including the trial and political murder of the aforementioned Captain William Kidd in 1701. Obviously, Anson supported by the British law Lords, and most certainly, Richard Coote, aka Lord Bellemont, set the wheels in motion to arrest Captain William Kidd and have a kangaroo court, which was designed to have Kidd executed very quickly and being unceremoniously hung by the neck until dead for not giving up his very special Catalina secret or had refused to give up the early details of what was to become the 'Horseshoe Expedition' booty secrets. Kemp Hastings, on the other hand, witnessed the death of his Captain whom he had accompanied whilst walking alongside the hangman's pony drawn cart as Kidd and other scallywags and pirates were being taken from Newgate prison to the Gallows at Tilbury Point. Hastings had listened intently as Kidd slurred out his last drunken testament and wishes. After which Kemp Hastings had retired quietly and strategically lapsed into a certain obscurity over time but eventually resurfaced on the St Mary's Isle, Madagascar. It was also rumoured that he had headed for the Catalina coast along with members of the original crew from the Quedagh Merchant and together they scuttled the infamous pirate vessel aided by Pirates - Barleycorn, Lamley, Jenkins, Loffe, Owans, and Parrott, who were all delivering on a pirate arrangement to avenge the untimely death of Captain William Kidd. Hastings finally semi-retired to St Mary's island and it was either to solve the early elusive **DM code** or had protected its real secret whilst working under the watchful eye of the ancient order, the Priory Of Sion or the Knights Templar, thus reaping the just rewards in the process and leaving the Infamous **DM Code** in the public domain for Anson to cogitate over. And this storyline may well have been his own death bed confession.

- A Latin translation is - et in arcadia ego - perhaps states, I keep God's Secrets or I am here. But the question is - who or what does this actually relate to?

The facts around this message are mixed and we must remain mindful that the two pieces of artwork connected to this ideal are not the same – Nicolas Poussin's two paintings are the original and Anson's copy modelled in relief as the third one, of which should be treated as very suspicious as the origin of the message. But the question we should really be asking is which version hides the real secret? We understand that George Anson had added his own particular bent or personal twist to the message and that he as a person may never have known what the real answer was - in the first place, or conversely, he did? Therefore, as a marker, we can find sitting within the vast grounds and gardens of good old Shugborough Hall, a rustic arch housed within the Greco - Romanesque splendour surroundings in the beautiful capability brown landscape that may or may not serve a great purpose. A place of peace where we can find the relief copy of the 'Shepherds Inscription', or at best guess a copy of Poussin's famous fine artwork, which basically depicts a woman and three shepherds in a graveyard where we can observe that two of the shepherds are pointing directly at a tombstone with a suggestion alluding to or explaining a certain point or location?

The wording elegantly carved into the tomb facia panel says: '*Et in arcadia ego*', which can be translated as 'I am', even in Arcadia, and we should also note that an extra tomb or ossuary is an addition that also displayed on this panel denoting a second sarcophagus sitting on top of the main feature. Therefore, we have to ask the question as to whom this second smaller sarcophagus belongs to. Which is still a certain bone of contention or set of bones for further discussion. We could stretch the sinews of our imaginations further and outline each figure demonstrating that a map of the African or South America continent could be superimposed across the work and that makes a certain level of sense if you were a Maritime or Naval oriented person. But this in itself appears too obvious in the DM case as Anson knew all his peers and crew could map read, and deciphering the DM code in this simple way would be far too easy for them to solve. Nicolas Poussin had also clearly painted two figures with heads, one showing a smiling curly-haired man and the other bearing a likeness to that of a mythical character, or man, or the horned Greek God, or perhaps even Pan himself, and all completed in splendid alchemic colours that could be deemed a code in itself in context. Below this plaque carving, we will find the mysterious eight (8) letters in a row which are encased between two letters a 'D' and an 'M', hence, the DM code reference.

(10 letters total). In this context, it may mean – **Dis Manibus** or Dedicated to the shades or shadows.

O.U.O.S.V.A.V.V
D M

CHAPTER SEVEN

'Nicolas Poussin's real genius'

The scene depicted in Poussin's **'Et in Arcadia Ego'** is a real atmospheric moment in time and certainly alludes to a suggestion that these heralds came together to signify an important message that would be conveyed to the outside world over the centuries that ensue, or in essence, could be a great discovery waiting to be discovered, perhaps of a religious tomb located in the mountainous regions of Greece. Albeit ironically captured much earlier is a predetermined written piece by the poet Virgil, which seems to be more by desire than by default. Virgil had written a poet named Eclogues consisting of many verses and appears to deal with death and the passing of the human soul, which may have been a burial set in the land of Arcadia, and could be deemed to be steering the reader towards the goals of happiness and enlightenment. We can discover that in a predetermined context in this artwork by Nicolas, we are momentarily reminded of an earlier artwork by another artist named Guercino. And Nicolas Poussin would have been more than familiar with the artist and his work as it reflects the work Et in Arcadia Ego in similar content and meaning, and the picture clearly touches on the subjects of both **death and mortality** in their own depictions, thus, highlighting the fact that Poussin's work also highlights a significant **'shepherd'** who may have been entombed in this location. We could, of course, hypothesise and raise the ultimate question of which one. Either **Jesus or John** the Baptist, or conversely great secrets as the given subject matter, but this will of course remain a serious 'bone' of contention for scholars and historians to debate.

Having left the Captain to his own devices, Kemp sat down in a quiet part of the vessel and removed the ledger and some maps from his satchel, followed by a rolled-up vellum scroll that depicted a sketch of the painting by the infamous Poussin, and he quizzed the work with an open mind whilst trying to decipher what the real mystery of this thing actually was, albeit he was amazed to find once again the same ten letters had been written across the front of the drawing. He had no idea that when he had stolen the documents from the desk tops and sea chests, they contained such informative documents and maps. He then ran his fingers over the crouching figure and traced the etching, '**Et in Arcadia Ego.**' 'So, I am here.' He whispered to himself as he accepted that someone was dead in the tomb, but who? Perhaps the tall female figure, the grieving widow, albeit she was elegantly clad in a rich dress and appearing to be sympathetic in her thoughts. Perhaps she was not the grieving widow at all but a sister or lover, but the interred was certainly an earthly bound person until their time of demise. Had he stumbled on something fantastic and would this conundrum lead a person or colleague for deception, or would he bring someone along to another graveside to remind them that he is in fact deceased? No, that would not be right. He recalled thinking that Kidd was not that intelligent, although he was very devious, and looking back over the sketch of poussin's work, the Pirate placed himself in the sandals of the two other characters in the scene, each person leaning over and pointing to the lettering as if reading out the letters aloud for no one to hear, but only to observe. The juxta position of these two biblical characters were quite balanced and mirrored their stance as he could see that the elbows and knees of the two central characters seemed to be strategically placed. Hastings almost choked when within his mind's eye as he could literally see a transparent map or an outline of the continent of the Americas and it was quite evident to the casual observer that he was a simple pirate and was certainly not aware of things such as the '**golden ratio**' or the serious geometry and math applied to such great artwork.

Although in his mind, this was still a copy of the original painting that Nicolas had completed. And it may be that the subsequent copies or additions to the painting may have had a subtle effect on the part of the artist as he grew in his understanding of both art and religion as time unfolded and the message that art could bring to the modern 17th century world at large, but obviously, he was oblivious to the fact that the work would create such a storm into the middle of the 21st century.

In his current mood, Hastings had relaxed somewhat, thinking that the sketch actually possessed a relaxing scene and set a tone of peace and almost changed his current mood for the moment, as being the casual observer witnessing a revelation, and wondered what the real colours would have looked like in the original work. Hastings laid the sketch on the table top and placed a few items at each corner to keep it flat. He thought that a simple map could be laid over the sketch and one could trace the outline of a continent, providing they knew the start point of the legend. He then started pointing with his index finger at the drawing and quite literally copied the figure in the sketch, then stopped over the 'R' in the script. He then searched the satchel and removed Kidd's map, the same map that Kidd had received on his earlier voyage from the young Ubilla. Placing the two together, he realised that they were not of the same dimensions, but he could use fancy guesswork and crack the code. Having no clue about what the "R' actually stood for, he guessed it would be a point where one could adjust or rectify numbers or letters or source the point of origin of the marker. Placing the map over the sketch Hastings lined up the middle of the map with the letter 'R' and found to his amazement the feint lines that had been drawn on the map actually fitted the sketch and he could see what he thought was a possible latitude and longitude. He observed that a small scale had been written down the right-hand side of the page and resembled the matrix that he had shown Kidd regarding the way to decipher the code using the alphabet, although he struggled as to why the code started at twelve (12) and remembered that Kidd had stated that many secret societies operated many versions of the same code. He looked at the letters again and found that the number nine (9) was indeed the letter 'D' and the letter 'M' was the number one (1). It was clear that these two numbers sat below the level of the letters and could be deemed the (Latitude). He then deciphered the remaining code using the matrix and the DM Code together and ended up with a grid reference. Hastings grabbed his quill and started to scribble into his notebook and began copying everything he could.

A	B	C	D	E	F	G	H	I	J	K	L	M	N	O	P	Q	R	S	T	U	V	W	X	Y	Z
12	13	10	9	8	7	6	5	4	4	3	2	1	13	14	15	16	17	18	19	20	20	21	22	23	24

D 9 – M 1

Lat O14 - U20 - O14 – S18- V20 – A12 – V20 – V20 Equals. **138 Degrees**

With the D and the M in the frame, coupled with the reference, Kidd had become aware that this knowledge would easily get him killed if the Black Lodge discover any of this was real and he knew the British were behind this drive to find the wealth and claim it as theirs. And the numbers 19 deg South and 138 North were certainly never going to be forgotten and made perfect sense when he quizzed the findings against the Ubilla sketch. The Ubilla sketch also had Hebrew lettering scribbled across the top and

Hastings simply knew this was more references and they would have to be translated. And what the RIO GRANDE had to do with sea charts was to push his level of logic to its optimum, but after a little thought and by simply using the English alphabet method he had used with Kidd earlier, he was surprised to find that the numbers also made sense apart from being fewer letters in Hebrew, and the first letters were RIOGA - RIO 42 Longitude and GA 71 Latitude.

As Hastings trawled through his notes, he had sketched what he thought was a fair interpretation of where the codes seemed to be pointing to and he had discovered that the Trinity or the words that Anson had written down in the HMS Wagers ledger were, in fact, the point where three intersections occur and this was the Ceros Tres Puntas note in Kidd's paperwork as well, but of course, there are no hills at sea and, therefore, could only mean reckoning, and that's where Hastings thought about the 'R' albeit this was all still guesswork and he would have to engage with Kidd to sense check what he thought was the most interesting thing that he had ever discovered.

CHAPTER EIGHT

'DM - 1696'

Captain Kidd had set sail on his special assignment with a crew that was predominantly made up of mixed races. His ship's log had recorded that he had five Dutchmen, seven Scotsmen, two Frenchmen, one African, two Welshmen, and a range of Englishmen from all parts of Britain. The essential disciplines according to Kidd were the cook, carpenters, surgeon, baker, gunsmith, joiner, cordwainer, and jeweller. The remainder of the crew were, in essence, labour and Officers. The ship's log recorded that the ages of the crew differed greatly from young apprentice sailors at around twelve years of age to sixty years of age. And, Kidd had clearly stated that Richard Barlycorne would be his next selected apprentice and made great efforts to ensure the lad had a career ahead of him, whether that was in piracy or naval application remained an outcome to be seen.

Having signed articles dated 10th September 1696 on the Adventure Galley, the crew knew that they would be under strict rule. Kidd had assembled the crew on the after deck and ran through the detail of articles prior to this adventure and wanted no uncertainty in the crew, especially as he knew that his future cargo was going to be potentially high-end. 'Listen up all you sea dogs that have signed the articles, welcome aboard. I don't demand much from my crew just one hundred percent loyalty at all times and if you die in any way during your service, then I will personally make sure you are buried in honour either at sea or in the backyard. So, dry or wet, you will be looked after. Therefore, that brings me onto the smaller of print in articles for you lubbers that don't read or write. I will shout out loud and clear that in any medical cases you suffer, there will be 600 pieces of eight for loss of an eye, leg, or arm, or conversely, you could opt for six able slaves to feed you a constant barrage of ale and bread until you die. And if we do successfully sail, then, gentlemen, the prizes are that each man would receive an extra 100 pieces of eight as his bounty loot, but before you all go running off and buying your houses and horses, be very clear that any dis-obeyance of any command from any of my Officers, yea shall lose full share or receive corporal punishment, and if any of you lilly livered rats show signs of cowardice, especially during a healthy engagement, then you will still lose your share. But if you are drunk at the time of engagement, that's also loss of share if prisoners are not on board.' Kidd stopped yelling and leaned up against a backstay post and nodded his head, then continued, 'And the worst crime of all being mutiny, you will not only lose your share but we will serve corporal punishment or we get you to eat three full meals served up by Tee Chow our chief cook before noon. Now, personally, I think I would rather be keelhauled than suffer that kind of fate, but again, gentlemen, be very clear that mutiny and deception or fraud will be treated as a very serious crime on this vessel. Again, welcome aboard, and let us make ready for Chile. As Kidd and his crew set sail, a man called 'Warren' was not a very happy man at all as Kidd had also just borrowed the Adventure galley with an arsenal that could and would engage any Royal Navy frigate or man at war and win. After several days at sea, the Bosun had engaged the skipper and was asking for help to repair the several leaks and damage that occurred during the voyage, knowing that they were going to be approaching the Cape of Good hope shortly when the seas would be unrelenting. Kidd agreed and set six able bodies to assist the Bosun.

During the voyage, there were many bouts of cholera, scurvy, and one suicide had occurred and the crew was somewhat diminished by at least one-fifth. Kidd gave thought to his previous excursions that he had conducted and dwelled on the death of Moore again, an issue that was giving him concerns that his crew may think him a calibrated murderer, but he also knew that both the Quartermaster Walker and Gunner Moore were already bad apples on the crew, and it wasn't as a result of the fact that they had boarded the Mary and stole her cargo, it was mainly because they had both denied the orders of the Captain under the articles convention and quite clearly disobeyed command directly from him and had run amok and were very guilty of both torture and maiming of innocent parties in the process for which Kidd would not accept. Nevertheless, the Adventure Galley was now bound for Chile and would arrive in ten weeks sea time maximum if the winds, waves, and weather were favourable, and of course, the skipper knew the vessel had sufficient beer and food on board to keep the motley crew under control for the duration. But, unknown to the crew, less for two colleagues, the vessel already carried in her hold sixty pounds of gold and silver and a cargo that really belonged to the East India Company and other goods, which Kidd had decided was his get out of jail card as an offering should the world of treachery turn against him, and he could bribe his way to a pardon if needed.

On the 12th June, the Adventure galley had reached the Northern side of the warm archipelago waters of the Juan Fernandez islands, and having dropped anchor, she waited for three days before a lone ship named the 'Unicorn II' had been sighted by one of the crews on the far horizon. Kidd retired to his bunk and made ready for the meeting with the ship's captain.

- Cargo hold: Boxed: Sixty pounds of gold and silver, Baled goods, saltpetre, silks, weapons comp: sixteen swords and eight pistols, estimated value - £30,000.

By early evening, the Adventure Galley was sitting in one fathom of water, and Kidd and his vessel crew were making final preparations for the visit of their esteemed explorer and visitor. The Adventure Galley was surrounded by four very distinct merchant ships, each ship easily had a minimum of forty cannon and would sink the Adventure within seconds if they decided to open fire. To the fore was the Unicorn II sitting proudly at one cable length and was stemming the vessel with two forward cannons trained directly onto the forecastle of the Adventure Galley, and to the port side sat the 'Grifon' with full crew leaning over the bulwarks watching for any signs of aggression. At the starboard side sat the 'Capitana' and where the Captain was being made ready to board the vessel and meet the infamous Captain Kidd. Sitting two cable lengths abaft of the Adventure sat the 'Pinnacio', but she was too far away to inflict any damage should a healthy engagement ensue, but war was not on the cards today for any of these gentlemen. It was a Sunday and even in these remote parts of the world at sea or anywhere else on the planet, faith was always respected, the ships First Officer had conducted a very short and sweet sermon and ended by telling the crew that they will all eventually reach heaven and their many sins and transgressions will be absolved as soon as the decks were made ship shape and the gun bays were scrubbed. Kidd had already left the confines of his cabin and had donned his best uniform attire and presented himself clean, shaven, and somewhat presentable, with his leather bandolier crossed over his left shoulder, which held two pistols in their make-shift holsters ready for quick action, and as a contingency, he kept by his side a fair-sized sword, and in his inner jacket, he carried a short-handled sabre. Kidd smiled at himself in the reflection from the poor excuse of a mirror whilst contemplating how he was going to handle his notorious visitor.

As he stepped onto the decks of his vessel, the first thing that immediately struck Kidd and Hasting's attention was the huge emblem that was spread across the mainsail of the 'Capitana'; it was the easily recognisable insignia of the Knights Templar of Malta. The Captain of the Capitana was a fair-sized man who had donned a hybrid mix of Spanish and French uniforms for the occasion; his overcoats were panelled with blue and red patches and the high neck collar was black, with a trimming of gold braid that ran around the collar seam. General Ubilla was a stout man with rather hairy hands and his beard was neatly cropped and short. He had long, black curly hair and had two golden rings in his left ear to ensure that his burial costs were catered for, and what appeared to be a tattoo across his chest, which could be seen as his open cotton shirt hung loosely under his waistcoat. On his head, Ubilla supported a black tricorne or three-cornered hat with a single red coloured feather stuck in the left side; the odd design of hat by default would act as a water guttering in times of heavy rainfall and the brim remained free of rain; sadly, the shoulders would become saturated with rainwater. But in foreign countries, such head dress was becoming a new trend.

The remainder of the crew of the Capitana appeared mostly to have donned woollen skull caps on their heads coupled with loose-fitting cotton shirts and shortened trousers or short slops and the more seasoned few had placed odd coloured head-scarves on their heads and draped around their necks and had donned loose-fitting short blue and red overcoats that sat nicely over the waistcoat type jackets. The crews had begun mingling together and the Captain's had held their special meeting. The Officers quarters of the Capitana was very lavish and Kidd took time to survey the ornate wood work and the splash of colour that lit up the quarters. 'This is a nice bunk,' retorted Kidd as he accepted a glass of fine French cognac from the Esteban Ubilla. The General cocked his head to the left and spoke, 'Yes, I suppose it is. I don't really take much time to enjoy the splendour of one's surroundings, but I do ensure that the crew bunks are ship shape and every man has his space and his rations. If you keep them orderly, they soon learn what a great ship can really be, and not some two-piece of eight French frigate that I would not let my pigs live in.' Kidd toasted the Captain. 'To a scholar and a gentleman of integrity, there certainly ain't many of us left with those qualities, you know.' Ubilla drew his moustache through his thumb and forefinger then spoke, 'So, I suppose the reason we are here, Mister Kidd, is that I have something that has been entrusted into my care, it is a map and a few letters that seem to have the English Navy in a big uproar; they seem to think it's a treasure map belonging to one Juan Fernandez who was an explorer in his day, and an excellento naval navigator who may have discovered great riches, and there are rumours that say that this is the eternal resting place of Mary Magdalena, but I doubt it very much. Anyway, I am thinking that you are Privateer and you are under a Royal letter of Marques against the French. Well, in my country we don't think that's a big problem and therefore I think we could come to an arrangement. So what if I said, six of your cannons, twenty pounds weight in gold and silver and some of your little piglets for lunch and two hundred oranges would that be an offer you would consider Mister Kidd; after all, both of us know that the risk involved in finding this 'booty' could end up being no more than a chicken hunt in a fox farm. I have heard that the British are also looking for this map, so it's too dangerous for us to keep, so what do you say?'

Kidd contemplated for less than twenty seconds and made his decision then commented: 'The letters and a couple of those bottles of Cognac, and we have a deal.' Kidd spat on his hand and offered it to the skipper who had also spat on his own hand, then they both clasped hands and smiled. 'Deal, now let us have a few more ales before we set sail.' Once the transaction was complete, a few drinks were had by both Captain Kidd, the young Ubilla made their departing gestures, and the respective vessels were underway. Captain Kidd had left the Chilean waters as stealthily as he had arrived but close on his tail was a rogue British navy frigate of the Black Lodge destined to bring the crew of the Adventure Galley to Justice. But that was not going to happen today as the fleet under the command of Captain Estban Ubilla had seen to that little problem and just happened to be thirsty for war.

CHAPTER NINE

'Hastings and the Admiralty'

Captain William Kidd had no desire in bringing the 'Sloop' too close to the British Isles as he knew deep down that the Admiralty would take no time in bringing his vessel to account and attack his crew and then certainly arrest them all for simply being part of the 'sham' that was being recorded as the murder of Gunner Moore. After a few hours of coastal sea-faring, the vessel eventually reached a quiet inlet and sat just off the East coast and she had dropped her anchor. Meanwhile, Kemp Hastings and a couple of the crew had been tasked to 'run' ashore under the guise of traders and would work their way into old London town, albeit, they each knew they were on a quest that was already a very risky venture, and by design, the outcome would secure the future of the crew if the Admiralty would play ball with them. They had hatched the plan that both Kidd and Hastings had set in motion. In the interim period, a second crew had gone ashore to source food stuffs and ale for the pending journey onwards.

It was not long before Kemp Hastings had been very unceremoniously arrested whilst laid up in a local tavern, and his presence was now required at the highest level of the maritime authority in the land, the British Admiralty. He was to be quizzed by an interim Admiral of the Establishment called Adam Jacob

Duncan Senior, who was a man whose existence Hastings was very well aware of and was also a decorated Officer of the maritime fighting world. Duncan was another proud Scotsman hailing from the whaling city of Dundee in Scotland with a turbulent naval career and life behind him, some of which was well recorded in the annals of 16th century Naval war-craft. Hastings knew that he was up against some pretty tough intellectual competition should he decide to play the fool, but this man, Duncan, was no arrogant fool or moron either; he was dangerous to those who chose to oppose his rules. And as far as Admiral Duncan of the Red was concerned, he was simply trying to set the records straight and determine the actual account and events regarding the exploits of Captain William Kidd. And as a leading Naval Officer Duncan was determined to understand the reasons behind Kidd's infamous antics, not so much in and around the death of Gunner Moore, but more as to why had Kidd raised the French flag and was duping international ships to come alongside and be subsequently attacked by Kidd and his men. A tactic that was frowned upon unless the scope of attack was executed under the Letter of the Marque against French ships, but for Kidd to attack an Armenian or Lebanese vessel or any other nation's vessel in this manner was indeed an act of piracy and was not privateering. Details of which were mostly reported as being conducted under the blanket of high seas piracy. The modern press and authors of the 1700's print were virtually alive with many tales and stories specifically around the islands of Madagascar and the East India Company in both Sri Lanka and India, where the clandestine use of an illegal vessel was employed by the British Navy to attack ships at sea and plunder their rich cargoes whilst ensuring that the finger of blame would be pointed elsewhere. And, of course, most people knew that naval tactics can be shitty and a very damaging and dangerous business, including King William IIIrd who would certainly prosper financially from these adventures, albeit Hastings listened to the Admiral with great interest and surmised that Duncan was talking 'utter clap trap or he had been fed ludicrous amounts of lies and misrepresentation along with certain many dreamy notions', as all his details and uncorroborated ramblings were very inconsistent and mixed with very small parts of facts from reality, and that his overall picture and outrageous assumptions were simply skewed and premature in his delivery. His decision-making and assumptions were questionable, but sadly, his execution of dialogue whilst attempting to convince the young ex-officer to the fact that he was somehow complicit in this piracy scope of activity was almost laughable.

Duncan was an aged man in body but appears to be verging on immature in mindset or was drunk or he had been tippling before being introduced to Hastings. Although, in essence, he was trying to exploit the meeting and was simply seeking to gain a type of confession regarding Kidd's wrong doing, but Hastings was too quick for the old fox as he was not born yesterday and had more integrity than simply blabbing or telling stories out of school at the first opportunity, especially to rich self-serving whigs which he greatly despised so much, and had at this juncture chosen to play a double bluff with the old arrogant Admiral. For the young ex-officer, it was a decision he made to ensure that he did not, firstly, betray the one man who would most likely slit his throat in the middle of a card game just for the fun of it than obey the ignorant commands of the landed gentry and ship owners of old London town, and secondly, the prospect of facing a civil trial would be a walk in the park compared to dealing with Captain Kidd directly who was certainly not a man to be betrayed either, let alone contemplate turning renegade or go against his trust today, or any other day for that matter—in fact, deceit was not on the cards regarding Kidd at all. And thirdly, the Admiralty were not to be dismissed either as they would certainly make life very painful indeed and could create a certain hell for him should they desire, or at the very least make his current existence very unpleasant indeed; they would, of course, tolerate his antics until it was time for him to 'swing high' from the wooden gallows as a traitor to the crown. Either way, Hastings had to play a very strategic game of words and gestures with his incumbent interrogator, especially if he was to gain any trust from the establishment. And therefore, he very cunningly chose his next few comments very wisely whilst responding to the monotonous strategic soft skills line of questioning.

The Admiral had stood up and now faced Hastings and was staring directly into his eyes. 'So, tell me, Mister Hastings, your accomplice, this Captain Kidd, surely, you sir, this renegade, and deserter, I would think that Kidd should have strung you up by the throat and very high from the yard arm well before now. So, tell me please, if you will, what is it that you have done that warrants his undue protection because if he knew you were here today, then you are already a dead man? Especially for turning on him like this in such a slap dash manner. Or perhaps you are here for other reasons? And what I mean by that is that you have already escaped from his control; if that is the case, I should say, my dear fellow, sitting in an ale house mid-day is hardly the 'brig or the cockpit' now, is it? Which in the eyes of the Admiralty is almost a collusion of brothers in arms, and especially with such a famous pirate could be deemed a mutinous act, almost complicit, irrespective of who one's captain and commander may well be. And, I should also wager that this is definitely not an act becoming of a British Naval Officer or Merchant one in the ranks ex-service or otherwise I would think most irregular, to say the least. But tell me why do you think Kidd has let you live thus far?'

Hastings pondered on the question for quite a bit of time before applying a very clear and succinct answer, 'Well, sir, normally I would have to agree with you there, that the why? It is indeed a complex and very difficult conundrum to answer, and I should say that Captain Kidd is a very unpredictable man and can be deemed a 'cad' and he is most certainly a certified scoundrel, to say the least, and yes, I agree, perhaps, I should be lying in the gutter or facing tits up somewhere feeding the crows, or as a consequence of law should be hanging on high from the nearest gallows. But here is my point, the man does have certain qualities that I almost admire and his unique style of leadership happens to be one of them, but let's face it, Admiral, he was trained by the British Navy, as I was, and he is, of course, a very 'loose cannon' indeed, but firstly, Admiral let me be so bold to explain and to inform you, sir, that whilst we were in the East Indies territories trading various livestock in a small insignificant port town on the Isle of St Marie, we became heavily embroiled in the most horrific of bar room brawls, it was a nightmare. It was a complete fracas, to say the least, where a few local unwelcome townsmen had decided to try and steal our coin, and to be quite blunt, and by sheer default, I actually saved Kidd's life during this particular bar room brawl. Just as one of his attackers was about to run the Captain through with a very long cutlass sword, that was when I intervened, because I watched on as Kidd lay semi-unconscious over an upturned table top, having been clouted with a rather large pewter ale jug from behind. He simply could not defend himself at this time, and, as I believe, I do have my honor and integrity to maintain and preserve but also knew in myself that no self-respecting ex-service British officer of the King William's Navy or any man of integrity would permit such a tragic low-level scum thing like murder under these circumstances to take place, especially out of turn where one was also very vulnerable, now, would they? But I do grant you, sir, it may have served society better if I had let this assailant kill Kidd and let him die like a dog in the gutter there and then. No, sir, not me, not Kemp Hastings, and therefore, to ensure my own self-preservation, I took it upon myself and lashed out and shot the attacker cold dead in one shot. One piece of heavy ball shot straight through the head right between the eyes, sending him cascading through the bar room window and out onto the rowdy street of a village somewhere in Madagascar in a hail of shit and feathers, I should add. You see Madagascar today is a very dangerous and unruly place. I would not venture around Madagascar in any uniform because one would simply not last five minutes as the place is infected with hairy-arse smelly pirates, vagabonds, scoundrels, and deviants from all countries across the globe and they can be found on every alley or hut corner and at every turn, especially the cemetery.

'The old bone yard is getting a bit overcrowded these days, but, sir, did you know that 'Kidd' already has a grave marked in the cemetery in New York with his name on it (and yet we both know that he is not dead)? Maybe he has a couple more graves dotted across the globe, who knows? And that's a bit odd, don't you think Admiral? So, all I can say that it was after this encounter that things between us got a little more relaxed for a while and then things became a little messier and complicated for me as Kidd began to trust me. You see, Admiral, it was due to Kidd's spontaneous bouts of anger and his thirst for revenge that drives his anger, mainly due to his open hatred of most things irrelevant. Because trust me, sir, I know him reasonably well. Kidd craves protection and lacks the moral trust of anyone, but he has no option these days as finding loyal crew is difficult, although he keeps harping on about 'a mission from god'; he says that he knows where the riches of the church are located, and he says they are in a secret location, or in several key locations across the globe, but there are artefacts that must be protected at all costs, and he needs good men to help him and protect these articles of faith and demands trust and loyalty from those close by. He also requires those men around him to remain secret within reason and to protect him at all costs. The auld Scots saying is very true as being 'thick as thieves', and this sentiment rings true with Kidd and his entourage, but this one virtue of trust of certain people sits within this horrible tyrant's uncalibrated nature, and I feel is still his only finest virtue. And he himself holds a certain style of loyalty to those that he himself has nurtured. You see, Captain Kidd is not ignorant, nor is he a high seas nightmare of a Captain to work or sail with; in fact, he is not this so-called swashbuckling murdering mutineer we all seem to be hearing about. But on the other side of the coin, if we take Blackbeard as an example one of the worst of them all, Captain Henry Morgan amongst many others, well, in my reckoning, they are all just common criminals of the worst kind. These are evil men living by evil standards, and I do believe also that the global perception of the man called Kidd is very much tainted by politics and very much distorted in its pitch – especially when compared against these other vagabonds, and what I mean by that is that he, Kidd, is perhaps one man that would strike you down as soon as he spits at you, but this depiction by the mass media and most likely driven by the lawmakers of the land is very distorted and false, and certainly one-sided. No, Admiral, I must say that the man is rationale in thought and can be a very cold and calibrated individual at other times, and let us remind ourselves again that he was still highly trained by the British Admiralty as I have already intimated. No, Kidd was a level-headed skipper whilst working under the British flag and I wager that you will struggle to find a better Captain by default in your current ranks, and that factor in itself makes him more of a serious adversary for you to contend with than you would ever imagine.

'But please, Admiral, do not underestimate Kidd's warring ability or strategy either. As a war technician, he is logical and can be cruel, kind, loyal, disloyal, or indeed trustworthy. You see, sir, I don't trust him one iota myself, not one tiny little bit, and I don't think he trusts me either, but he seems to need or want me around for this purpose of doing 'Gods work', which is driving him to the point of almost distraction, and sometimes he provides me with sparse or scant details as to where his treasures are hidden are, let's say near to Madagascar on the Eastern side of the islands, or sometimes the Northern side. I only know that some of his extreme cache of riches are secretly submerged in some very shallow waters off a small island near Madagascar island, or in one of the inlets. He has mentioned the far-off Chilean islands of Juan Fernandez but he is foxy, sly, cunning, and highly deceitful. But since our recent encounter, and untimely meeting with Blackbeard and his entourage in Algiers—which I should say was a meeting that resulted in yet another fracas or bar room fiasco and what now seems so long ago—Captain Kidd's attitude had changed greatly. I suspect something had scared him as he seemed very disturbed. I saw it in his eyes, he feared Blackbeard greatly and almost withdrew himself out of sight, skulking away like a mouse encountering a large cat. I can tell you that his whole outlook towards the preservation of his own life had changed since that day. And I should say, sir, that he was very disappointed by the actions and the ill decision making by this Admiralty office, especially in their efforts to protect him under the crown. But when he tracked Blackbeard down the first time in the East Indian colonies for this office, well, sir, he was not supported by the British naval department or the political offices of the East China Company either, to say the least, he was absolutely livid by their lack of support from there on afterwards. So, as a direct result, he has decided to wreak revenge. Blackbeard, I think, was the only one person that Kidd would not want to encounter face to face, but I would say that he may be even be seen as Kidd's nemesis, and I can tell you, Admiral, I physically watched as Kidd literally skulked silently into the back drop of the tavern, and he escaped or evaded any chance of a direct encounter with the man. And yet he could have killed him on this meeting, but he chose not to. And I personally think you gentlemen here within this establishment are most likely responsible for 'turning' Captain Kidd against yourselves and the structure rank and file of this fine naval establishment because you had sadly failed to manage him correctly if you pardon my directness Admiral; he is now a model and fine example of a great testament to failing management, mainly because you have tried to have him killed recently by using Moore as an example. Well, to be quite honest, he is not going to serve Britain with any favor now, is he? And that's for sure. So my immediate thoughts are if and when he finds the opportunity to dispense his own kind of rough justice towards the Naval ranks—and he will—well, Admiral, he will execute on sight and any further retribution in the eyes of Captain William Kidd will be aimed at King and country and their many global representatives. He will lash out unceremoniously at law and order and again trust me, sir, he knows and understands only too well that he has by all accounts very much exiled himself from the landed gentry. And I believe simply because we were serving officers together in the early stages of our careers, but I am sure that if I 'err', he will show no quarter and have me lynched.

'Therefore, I feel that because each of us served together on His Majesty's Vessels, I personally think he does not feel the need at this juncture to have me strung up from the yard arm just yet, and that, sir, was to answer your earlier question as to why I am alive today. You see, to him, this would be seen as a mark of rage or cold revenge and as I said earlier he has amazing leadership qualities and his methods are very much obscure, but instead of slicing and dicing me up into tiny pieces of cat meat and feeding me to the fish, would you believe me if I told you that he actually sent me here to London and to that particular ale house as his messenger, knowing full well that your henchman and press-gang were around? He also knew that you were watching us, but the question you should be asking yourself is how did he know?

'Perhaps, he thinks I am able to negotiate the protection of his life in a swap for secret critical information, or it could be the fact that he could direct the Officers to a certain amount of acquired Holy riches from Peru or in the islands of Chile that sits beyond your imagination, and maybe that is the only real reason why I am still alive today, as he knew, either way, I would eventually seek an audience with the Admiralty at some point or they would seek one with me. And look, so soon after I hit the streets of London, Admiral viola, here we are. May I remind you, sir, and indeed the silent court listening within or behind these lavish walls regarding the background around Captain William Kidd and his dastardly efforts, he is a very able seaman, and he is by all accounts a swashbuckling seafarer and can be a very ferocious fighter and yet he can and will be your worst enemy or conversely your best friend. You see, he has never really disliked any of his own crew unless, of course, they turn against him or execute mutiny, and recently an incident occurred that you may or may not be aware of in that context. We recently watched on as the Admiralty engaged tyrants to take his ship from his very command, especially such a short time after Robert Culliford snatched his ship from him in Antigua. And this event regarding William Moore occurred just a short time back, of course, you may already know that, and yes, sadly a death had occurred in the ranks. Captain Kidd had never intended to kill or disfigure any of his crew at this time, but in a fit of angered rage against the crown and with the deepest of disappointment, he struck out in the name of preservation to save his own skin as the gang leader, in this case, was his single target. A gunner no less, William Moore, a key figure on board any vessel, and the one man with his mindset on Captaincy of the vessel, and as a consequence was struck in the head with a bucket, and we now understand that he was acting under specific instructions from an unknown source. But, we know differently today that it may have been this very office. Nevertheless, let me inform you that having undermined Captain Kidd and challenge his authority in this way in front of his crew, well, it was a foregone conclusion that the obvious casualty was the ring leader and very unfortunate individual. So please let me remind you also that the Captain could have quite easily pulled out his musket and shot his assailant in self-defense, but he did not; instead, he launched a metal bucket at the man, and, unfortunately, it hit Moore on the side of the head, and sadly much added to his demise. And yet Kidd now fears today that he will be unfairly trialed and executed.

'So here is the conundrum for you to consider, he has played another important card mainly due to the nature of this secret cargo of riches and a batch of ancient Holy treasures that he knows exists and that he appears to have access to, having acquired sketches and maps from a chap called Ubilla something, and quite bluntly states that if you attack him at any time, he will simply burn and scuttle the 'ship' with all its precious religious riches in the hold without hesitation. You see, Admiral, when we planned to originally scuttle the Quedagh Merchant, there was also plenty of riches still on board her to consider and they still remain there today. When we took the ship in 1698, her cargo included not only 1200 bales of muslin, calico, and other fabrics, along with 1400 bags of brown sugar, 84 bales of silk, and the great find of over 80 chests of opium, iron, and some silver, that haul, Admiral, was to all accounts in the value of approximately £50,000. And before, we sailed to Madagascar and took possession of a few barrels and chests full of jewellery, gems, and another French Pass. Captain Kidd had sold the cargo and provided his crew with their share; I could say that Opium and silks sold for £10,000 in gold bars then we hauled anchor. Mind you, Admiral, by this stage, the Adventure Galley was in a poor state and was leaking profusely, but Kidd had the vessel repaired and we sailed to a location that Kidd says will be the eternal resting place of the vessel. It is also known currently as the secret of the **'Cara at Catalina',** and, of course, the ship's log for the Quedagh Merchant contains all the sets of co-ordinates, including the intended or potential sinking location of the vessel.

'But you see, Admiral, if the authorities ever found out that the Cara was laced with silver and gold trinkets and cargo that any pirate was prepared to die for, and trust me, sir, if any of the crew are placed in any such danger whatsoever, then I should let you know that there should not be any doubt whatsoever in anyone's mind that the vessel, if compromised, will be instantly scuttled. And all the crew know and have accepted that fact. And trust me, sir, Kidd is already planning the scuttling the 'Adventure Prize' in shallow waters near the coastal lagoons in depths so shallow that urchin divers can reach her hold in a single dive. And as there are many other deep lagoons in the world, of course, it will be very difficult or almost impossible to locate the actual location designated for the Cara. The same outcome will happen with any of his ships if the need arises, but I will only say that the Catalan Saints may guide you to the Quedagh Merchant when Kidd wishes it to happen. But please don't waste your time looking or searching as the lagoon identified as a second location for scuttling is many fathoms deeper and sits in the dark and muddy waters off a peninsula. Then there is part-two to think about and that is the man map itself to consider, a secret which is still very much hidden away as a fail-safe measure for Kidd's retirement planning—well, that is according to him. Somewhere in the Dominican Republic is a large chunk of the area to navigate as you know only too well, Admiral, and you should also know that only four men alive today possess one-quarter of a very special map drawn up and tattooed on their very skin for this very reason and purpose. Kidd had some very heavy dealings with traders in both Haiti whilst working out of Port au Prince and Port de Paix and he often remained there for weeks at an end, especially as he worked his high seas raids against the East India Company; it was said that the traders were in league with one another and would pass the journey maps to insider traders who would, in turn, pass these maps down to Kidd for a tidy sum of cash. Whereupon, Kidd would engage other secret members, especially in Santo Domingo, as it was rumored that Kidd had a very special treasure map 'tattooed' onto each one of his crew to stem any skullduggery and mutiny against him. There are four tattooed men – known as the man map, but if you capture

Kidd, you might have the names of people who hold a treasure map in its entirety, but I would suggest you capture his complete crew as you would have a better chance of success. I suggest capture Kidd first then keep the vessel crew together, but don't forget the Indian—the man that is in the middle of this unique strategy—he goes by the name of Coirgi or Baba to his friends and he works directly for the East India company; he is as corrupt as them all put together. He has lived for many years in Santo Domingo, but trust me, Admiral, he is very untrustworthy. I met him once and I did not take to his open brash and slap dash attitude nor his negativity towards foreigners either, although he does have a very strange hold over Kidd as well, maybe it's a secret Kidd is almost willing to die for but he is not of the man-map. And, Admiral, you may also find that the real 'treasure' is not simply sitting in full view as it were; shall we say that it will remain hidden in the distant future and may soon rest near to the carcass of the 'Adventure Galley.' There are rumblings that young Cornelius Patrick Webb is going on another journey to Chile, according to sources, and I do hear the vessel sails very soon or so I understand. Another global excursion off to meet Anson in the Bahamas, I would wager.

'Captain Kidd says his vessels will all be scuttled if attacked. Therefore, Admiral, just another potential location which I should warn you about, and that is where a second vessel is going to be moored then finally laid to rest according to Kidd, and what I hear is that it is about two fathoms of water depth just off the Eastern coast of Madagascar. Well, let us just say that is the Captain's new bargaining chip; he wants you to know that fact and, sir, as I said before, please do not underestimate Kidd, he is a man of his word, alas! I may fear that this next discussion may well be between Captain William Kidd, the Admiralty, the hangman, or at worst case, Davy Jones.'

The rear Admiral of the red took a long, hard view at the ex-officer and smiled, then started to strut around the office like a rooster on heat. 'So, my own thoughts are that you are going to support Captain Kidd in this madcap adventure to where ever on the planet it takes you and you will aid and assist him to scuttle this 'vessel' if need be whilst playing this game of deadly cat and mouse with us, are you?' Hastings smiled in unison with the Admiral as he spoke. Then he responded, 'What other choice do I have? I am indeed going to help him, sir, but certainly not for the same reasons you may be thinking. Every man has a price, as you fully understand.' The Admiral suddenly interrupted and spoke out of turn, 'And tell me, Mister Hastings, what is your price? What does it take to buy your loyalty or trust?' Hastings responded in a shallow but very firm tone, 'Me? My price, Admiral, is that I wish to live long and be happy and die a very old man and, of course, to prosper after all this complex affair is over. I do not wish to end up living my life like a sewer rat in old London town, running and hiding out of sight from every ruthless scallywag and pirate across the land. But, there is a difference between Kidd and I, Admiral; I am very much loyal to the country I call my home, and Scotland is my home, and I retain a certain level of respect for this office to some extent as this was part of my naval career origins. But I do also have a duty to the Order of the Knights of Malta and Santiago who hail from the Priory Of Sion at every juncture, and they have recruited my skills and involvement in acquiring and preserving of a few Holy trinkets and relics that have gone missing, and I will add, sir, that the Royal Society of London may wish to be repatriated with the very trinkets that Kidd may have already acquired, and I do have it on good authority that he has taken stock of something very significant. Kidd was talking recently about the Map of the Conquistadors and their Inca gold recently, but I am not sure if he intends to search for the booty in Chile or that he has already been there, as I have no idea what this single Holy relic is. But it may just be a special piece.'

The Admiral's attention span suddenly perked up and he quizzed Hastings a little more. He took a small piece of paper from his desk and clasped it in his fist. 'This Map you talk about, this coded thing, I take it that you know this is supposedly a conquistador map that leads to great biblical riches taken from King Solomon and the Incas many years ago, mister Hastings? But please tell me, why would a Captain like Kidd be interested in such a notion as to seek a treasure that has never been discovered so far away from his own territory, and against all the odds?' Hastings smiled and said, 'Ah, well, sir, that is easy to answer. Kidd is a pirate by heart and he can only see gold and silver as a reward, but I would imagine that he has no real inclination of the real worth of this trove nor does he know how to decipher the coded maps and secret alchemic symbols that accompany them. The gold and trinkets for me, on the other hand, are somewhat inconsequential to my actual cause and dare I may say that if all works out well, then both the Holy Order and the Admiralty may have this 'lot' for compensation for their efforts and support. But, presently, what matters most to me is that I have to preserve a single item, and with your blessing and support, of course, based on the premise that if I can be permitted to continue on my quest, I intend to deliver Kidd and his motley crew back to you at some point in time.

'But until then, I do ask that you provide me with your solemn word that Kidd and his crew will be given a fair and just trial bearing in mind that Captain William Kidd held a King's naval commission and a Letter of Marque, although he killed Gunner Moore by accident, which was not an act of evil hatred or aggression or one of malicious intent to murder, and in reality could be deemed self-defense. I know this because I was there to witness this very event when Kidd caught Moore with the bailing bucket. And if I may also be so bold, perhaps, sir, may I request some coin for myself to enact this discharge of these new secret duties? As His Majesty's Navy has still not paid my final salary of service for over two years now, sir, shall we say one hundred pounds, which of course, I will account for in every detail once I deliver the goods to you?'

The Admiral placed his right hand on the table-top, leaned forward, then responded, 'Well, Mister Hastings, you really do have some set of balls about you, young man. I will say that much, but tell me first of your understanding of this treasure trove, this Ophir, the so-called treasure of ancient kings, as I am sure that you are aware that Ophir is known as the city of gold and is reported to be located somewhere in Africa or could be found in Ethiopia itself. I hear that the Philipines or Malaysia is a fine choice of location for great wealth to be exploited but, personally, I am not convinced, but my money is on Chile. I know because I too have tried to discover great riches and sailed the seven seas. And you may or may not know, young man, there are great treasures in Ethiopia, biblical history thousands of years old, and the country states that even this ancient Ark of the covenant was supposed to be located there in the country. The Ark was initially hidden on an island Jewish settlement of Tana Kirkus in Lake Tana, and it remained there for seven hundred years and was re-located to a small village known as Axum. However, I am sure that the Queen of Sheba herself may have protected Solomon's wealth and God's holy relics in her tenure as Queen, having, of course, presented some of these riches to her husband, King Menelik, after he brought the Ark from the holy land, if you believe in the historical records. I am not sure that your Captain Kidd would ever get his head around this concept and consider this as an important issue in the moral sense of the word, as he seems to me to be an ignorant man when it comes to the church and religion. And you are certainly aware that we do have the unreserved resources to find you anywhere on the globe and we can also remove you and Kidd from existence if you decide to renegade on our plan.

But, yes, Mister Hastings, why? But my better judgement tells me to go along with this mad cap idea and notion of yours, albeit, I should also say that I do actually like you and that you might be of considerable help to us. I would simply ask that you locate the Conquistador's map and ensure that you deliver it along with Kidd and his crew to us here at the Admiralty. We do require a little assistance here with this undesirous problematic issue, but I will say that perhaps the Navy has made a great mistake in letting you go from the naval service, young man, as you do appear to have a kindred spirit and you possess a certain air of confidence about you. So, it's yes. I think we at the Admiralty can agree to your terms and request. Besides, we really do have little or no choice and we obviously need your help. You must make a decision, Mister Hastings. Decide to help us and stop rogue pirates such as Kidd from attacking the East India Company fleet as we cannot deal with them anymore, and of course an expectation that will form part of our agreement because they are costing us a literal financial fortune. And please tell that to Kidd when you next see him, would you? And, Mister Hastings, you have some property belonging to Captain Anson, but he will not tell us what it is, says it too secret to disclose, so perhaps can you shed some light on what he is looking for.'

Hastings smiled. 'Ah, sir, these are love letters. They are letters from a prominent lady in his social circle and alas, sir, I have sent them to the smokey fires in the sky, burnt them, sir. They are full of talk about flowers and love and butterflies. Anyway, they were not for any man to have in his possession and I think both parties are better off now that they are gone, sir.'

The Admiral puckered his lips and rubbed his waistcoat. 'Well, that is maybe, but secondly, young man, decide to give up your life as a privateer once this damn charade is over and consider returning to His Majesty's Navy for further service. I am sure you will be justly rewarded. But please first make your peace with your Holy Order and then with your God, after which you can return to this office when the time is right and we will make good on our word, and, Mister Hastings, I only promise you that much no more.' Hasting's semi saluted the Admiral then spoke, 'Admiral, I cannot guarantee that Kidd has the influence to stop other pirates from continuing their privateering affairs, but I would wager that the East India Company may not be as big a target as they think they are. I hear there is a rumbling that Malaysia and the Red Sea is becoming more of an advantage than that of the Barbary Coast, but until the Tunisians, Libyans, and the other Muslim countries get their act together, as I also hear that the Americans will most likely concentrate her naval efforts in a blockade or destroy the Barbary harbor areas, well, they will until they can gain safe passage of their trade routes. But who cares anyway as I hear a new American president will be elected soon and things will change.'

Hastings then left the office knowing full well that the Admiralty was never going to be trusted under any circumstances, but he did have one hundred pounds sterling in his trust to have some fun with, and yet sitting only a few miles north of the large city, the vessel 'Sloop' had already started to haul anchor and was awaiting the arrival of its new first officer ex-Naval Lieutenant Kemp Hastings as a new age Buccaneer and all-round scallywag.

CHAPTER TEN

'Rumbo'l Dumpling'

Kemp Hastings had stepped on board the merchant marine vessel 'Sloop' or the Adventure Prize to those in the know and he smiled a very broad smile. He gazed over the deck timbers and the tall main masts and absorbed the amount of ropes, rigging, and sails that stood before him. She was a very large and awesome vessel comprising of a few hundred tons of solid oak timbers and she stuck out proud against the other vessels that were quietly laid up against the long wooden jetty. Her sails and extensive rigging arrangement clearly stood out from the crowd as she was silhouetted against the bright sun and cloudless blue lazy skies; of course, her name plate was not so evident. The Adventure Prize was of a hybrid square-rigged and ad hoc designed merchant craft, albeit older in her overall construction, and yet whilst she was docked at the Northern end of the old jetty in the seaport appearing almost brand new and ready for swift action. A unique vessel with a chequered history and she had recently become another spoil of the high seas piracy program as far as ownership was concerned. And today she belonged to the newly styled Swashbuckling Buccaneer and devious Pirate -Captain, William Kidd esquire, a man who can boast as being an ex-Royal Navy Officer, entrepreneur, and Privateer at the same time, and was taking time to add pirate to his grand journey through life. It was after a few minutes of traversing the long alleyways and cabins that Hastings had soon found the Captain sitting in his quarters, knee-deep in old vellum parchments and an array of silver trinkets and jewellery strewn around his feet. The Captain was reading some documents that had been on the top of the chest and had tossed them about the deck space. The skipper had also supped a good skin full of pussers rum and appeared to be clutching his latest brand of gut rusting brews. Hastings smiled another broad smile and nudged the leg of the old table. 'My good god, Kidd, surely you cannot be serious about taking this piece of shit vessel as far as Nova Scotia again, are you? Well, surely not in the state you are in at the moment. Are you really serious? It will take a Sabbath of Sundays to reach Nova man, and even if we do make it beyond the Americas this time, we will surely meet Davy Jones underway.' Exclaimed Hastings handing over the piece of vellum with the rudely scribbled message from Kidd that he had received earlier in the week, it read: 'Find the 'sloop' off the East coast five miles southern end of walnut cove, find inlet cove at and we sail for Nova Scotia next convenient tide'.

Kidd sat quietly on the wooden stool and took a long stare back at his companion before speaking, 'Here you had better have a swig of this as you might need it when I tell you what we are going to do, and yes, to tell you that we are going to go to New Scotland, and yes in this vessel, but only when a convenient tide presents itself, probably in about five or six bottles time I should think.' He said pointing to the glass bottle on the table-top whilst still smiling. 'But, first, I need to clear my tarnished name. As you know, my anger and rage at times are uncontrollable, and I am certain that my outbursts will eventually cost me life or limb and that fact I know, and I understand only too well, my friend, but a turbulent crew needs quelling, and they need controlling with rapidity, a quick resolve be very quick when drawing the blusters or swifter with sword because there is no room for mutiny in my ranks, these dogs need sorting good and proper when these dogs rise, they must be put down without mercy, and well that response to nasty sailors takes a different kind of sea skill entirely. But if I don't seek my forgiveness and clemency from the Lord above before my death, my tortured soul will never rest. But first, I, no, no, that is 'we', my friend, we have a duty to do; we must hide this booty away from those many prying evil eyes, and only then after that action can we begin our new quest, which is just beginning with this voyage, because we have the most precious of cargo on board.'

Hastings removed his hat and placed it down on the oak table and rubbed his chin with his forefinger and thumb, then took the bottle from the Captain and took a very long swig of the rum, then responded, 'You know the Admiralty wants you dead? Duncan was very clear about that and believe me our chat was not a good one at all. You are certainly going to swing for killing Moore. Mind you, if Moore had struck you with that chisel rather than his fist then you may have had an eye patch by now.' Kidd gave out a murmur of laughter then nodded his head left and right in fair jest. 'Even though he was the ring leader and potential mutineer, but let's face it, you do have other deadlier enemies, my dear friend, to worry about. For starters, screwing up the ship Blessed William that was not a good tactic at all, then, of course, that intolerable Culliford, what a sneak thief. I knew he would turn out to be a complete bastard of a man. Then your partner in crime, Lord Bellemont, who will definitely screw you up. I tell you that for now, Captain, he is one not to be trusted; his eyes are too close together for my liking—I cannot take to the man at all. And then there are usual suspects, cutless swinging Tew, Morgan, Wake, Maze, Ireland, Sprigg, Howel, all your favourites.' Kidd smiled as Hastings read off the list then gulped at his rum. 'Are you finished yet? Yeah, well, they all have their own ruddy issues to deal with as well, don't they?' Hastings nodded again and continued reciting the details of his meeting with the Admiralty. 'Anyway, I get the impression that the Navy nor the courts will consider any of your evidence as credible and may not support in your favour and they will not reason with you either, and I do think they will not accept any excuses or reasons as to why you killed Moore. Gunners are a protected species! And they will say a good Captain will keep order at all times, and yes, don't tell me, I know it was an accident, but the monarch along with his overtly corrupt government, well, they will want your fat Scots to hide and head for skinning, not only for stealing from merchant ships within the East India Company but for turning their precious Navy into a sailing mockery in the eyes of the Maritime world at large. And the EIC want you dead as well, and that's where I think Bellemont comes in, as the East India people are on their financial knees thanks to you, even though they tried to set you up by sending Moore in the first place as disruption tactics. But you do remember your oath; if you work for the Admiralty, then you serve the Admiralty, and you serve the establishment until you die in your bunk, and you must die with your boots on. But sadly today, my friend, you are seen as a turncoat renegade, your Letter of Marque is null and void, the French ships are still free game, but the letters to attack the French flag, well, they won't matter now; we may as well attack the British flags. The King will surely make an example of you no matter what you do and probably me as well for that matter. King William, he is now Lord of the British Admiralty and he has political sway with the Americans, and you know he is bloody ruthless and he won't care that you are a Navy skipper either, he will have you on the gallows quicker than you can say 'Jack Spratt's left bollock'. The Admiralty will make you swing for eternity, and even more so, especially if you don't give them your booty. They can go suck fish eggs and eel lips as far as I am concerned. Anyway, skipper, may I ask a question? This biblical relic you talk about, if it is real, then I take it that it is not for any one single person to own, and as you say, it does not belong to one single country either. But belongs to a host of holy nations.'

The Captain took a very long deep shallow breath and spluttered out a few more words, 'It's not just the loot they want my lad, they are just greedy bastards, the whole lot of them; they don't care about faith or humanity, they are just a set of moronic self-serving greedy whigs, and look at me now deemed a pirate and I despise them all.

'It is 'The Holy Relics' that they want. They lust after the icons of Christian belief and the holiest relic that we, mister Hastings, will surely encounter very soon. But that cargo, my dear friend, is not going anywhere within one thousand miles of Briton's coast. You see, Mister Hastings (Ipsa Scientia potestas est') spouted Kidd like a university lecturer. 'Knowledge is power', that was once quoted by a Mister Francis Bacon himself. And, yes, another bloody pirate and in our world power is king in certain circles and the information about what is inside my head, my lad, along with my copies of some dodgy maps as well, they should see to that our existence is always protected and that's why you must come with me on this crusade and together we sail back to Nova, and do our deed for the Order. Although for now, my impending death can hang on just a bit longer if you pardon the pun. we are on a journey to serve the good lord above, but I need a trusty companion, I need a man whom I can trust beyond all others and one that will kill a fellow man to preserve what we are about to do. I cannot rely on these morons. Good men they once were...'

Kidd stood up and placed his left arm up against a large wooden beam that supported the deck head and then slugged back two swift large helpings of his Pussers rum, whooa'. He splurged and smiled. 'Now that is real man's rum.' Kidd would often make this comment after another (dead man) hit the bucket and shattered into many glass fragments. 'There is more where that comes from. Please call the galley rat, will you Mister Hastings? I want our ration assassin and chief sludge maker - Mister Rumbowl Dumpling - to muster us up a fine meal for us this evening, and be sharp about it Mister 'H'. We will actually dine this evening like real people; we will eat to celebrate our new venture. Now let me think, where did I stuff them? I do have some cutlery somewhere. We need to be eating with irons to assist us in the proceedings.'

The Captain fumbled around the cabin then suddenly stopped abruptly, he then shouted loudly whilst opening his cabin door at the same time and began yelling at the top of his voice down the narrow corridor. 'Tee Chow, ya Japanese tea brewing slanty eyed git. Get me a cup of yer finest brew water and I want Lieutenant Hastings to taste the eloquence of fine shrubbery steeped in hot water, then bring a few pussers along, and ask Mister Raddy Anka if he will clean my blunders, bloody pistols have seized up again. Thank you, Mister Chow, now choppity chop chop, jaldy jaldy, and I mean today ya lazy keel crawling weasel.' Hastings smiled at the elegant and charming tones of the skipper as he laid down his list of requirements. The Captain instantly turned swiftly on his mark and stared directly back at Hastings again. 'More pussers mister 'H' got to keep them on their toes you know because in my world once you break the seal you have to make the 'deal' with the devil that is, and slurp it all down; it sort of makes shit disappear.' Kidd raised his bottle again and he thanked Hastings for his efforts. 'Cheers and here's to you in our new endeavours in the art of swashbuckling.' Hastings smiled and raised his bottle for the second time, realising that Kidd was actually up for a partnership. And, responded with grace, 'To you, Captain Kidd, and may Scotland thank you for all your biblical interventions to whatever end that they may bring, and hopefully, in time the Admiralty realise their many mistakes and suffer the wrath of Davy Jones himself.'

Kidd then said, 'Hastings, so tell me something. When I was on the HMS Wager, I heard a story, well, it was more of a rumour than a story really, and that the HMS Wager had attacked a Templar ship called the 'The Unicorn I' and had looted their precious cargo which consisted of gold and relics, and part of this story was that another vessel the 'Adventure Prize' had intercepted the HMS Wager not long after near the Straits of Gibraltar. Of course, that was before I joined her a year ago and that seemed odd to me as I could not trace any evidence of the attack in the Wager's log book.' Captain Kidd raised an eyebrow and smiled a very cynical smile, then continued, 'That's because as far as we are concerned, it never happened, but let me tell you my dear friend, it did happen, that's why Anson was on board after it was taken and made secure by this crew; only five people on board know of the theft, and it was not exactly in the straits of Gibraltar, it was inshore near the West coast of Morocco and it was myself, Brassy and Grapeshot that had got aboard her in the early hours as the crew had been celebrating, and they were either all down with scurvy or were too drunk to notice our presence. Anyways, Captain Cheap was certainly drunk and that was to our advantage. But when we reached the cargo hold, there was a large box just sitting in the corner of the foc'sle, it looked like a treasure chest for silks and the like but this one was twice the normal size, but it had the words 'Ofir' written on one side, so we opened it up and we found an amazing thing. Well, this biblical object was simply too heavy to just pick up and walk away with, so Brassy and Grapeshot had a great idea and launched it 'south' to the deep six and out through one of the gun ports it went and landed into the deep. But still, I say we were lucky as most of the crew were still in the cockpit and the ship was quite literally deserted; we picked the relic up only two days later and the crew of the HMS Wager were none the wiser and that's why they will not really talk about it today because they lost one of the most important relics they will ever likely see. But whether Anson really knew if Captain Cheap had reported the total account of the haul is a matter for someone else to discuss.

'When we returned to the location to recover this object, we found it very quickly as it was only under ten feet of water under the keel, and in fact, you could actually see it glisten in the water. Luckily, though Brassy had attached a twine line with two-gun flags attached to one end, so the flags floated and they were just waiting to be lifted, but the funny thing for me is that could you imagine the faces of the Admiralty hierarchy if Cheap had informed them that they had found riches and were sailing to drop them off in London. And imagine the great scene when they opened up the box only to reveal two cannon balls roped together with twine, then one could smile with glee, fools that they are.' Hastings started shaking his head in disbelief. 'So you're saying that this rumour is true and the relics are here.' Kidd stopped supping and took a deep breath, saying, 'You will find out soon enough, my lad, but for now, it's pussers.'

As the night drew in, both Hastings and the Captain had taken their fill and five bottles of pussers and the empties lay as very dead men strewn across the cabin. Hastings had awoken in the middle of the night still in the skipper's cabin and almost able to focus on the bunk across the room only to find William Kidd snoring loudly and very unconscious. He stepped across Kidd's chair and one of the old sea chests and began making his way to somewhere quieter and could only smile as he haphazardly made his way to his cabin ensuring that for now at least Captain William Kidd was safe from not only himself but secure from any further wrong doing. In his mind, he somehow knew that the path of life is full of surprises and Kidd was certainly one of them. In those early days sea-roving was over in a short period of time often fate would sink a boat or scurvy would claim its victims.In the real world Captain Kidd had recruited perhaps some of the worst crew of cutthroats that any officer would have had to manage or deal with in any career path, but it was in Madagascar two years earlier in the village and local tavern that events changed for the worst. This village was not a very nice place to be at the best of times as every vagabond, murderer, thief, prostitute, untrustworthy crook, and scallywag had honed in on this one specific location to exploit the opportunity. It was also during the many voyages of the Merchant ship the Adventure Galley that we touch upon maritime life for the purpose of this voyage of fiction, and the vessel in question was a large merchant vessel boasting thirty-four cannon and weighing in at almost two hundred and eighty-four tons; she was a formidable vessel of the day and originally commissioned to rape and pillage the high seas on behalf of the British Navy, or the Admiralty, depending on your outlook. And she and her crew were to take care of high treason and piracy as she went along her way.

The obvious pomp and circumstance that once shone in the ranks of the naval crew had since dwindled away to mere tipping of the hat in ceremonial gesture, and formed part of old-style naval ceremony to keep an almost loyal standing on the decks, and not to mention that it was normally an action before any crew member was likely to challenge any authority figures, especially at this point. And an example is the actions of the ship's gunner William Moore, who tried to assault the captain and who only to his detriment discovered that this unruly act led to his own deathly demise; it was a very ill-conceived plan and was supposedly hatched by the British Admiralty. Although Moore had, in essence, failed to follow orders and wanted to attack another vessel under their French Marque, Kidd had reasons not to attack the vessel and Moore disagreed openly and undermined Kidd's authority in front of the crew; a fracas then broke out, resulting in the accidental death of William Moore. In the months leading up to taking the Vessel, the Quedagh Merchant, which incidentally was taken by brute force, Captain Kidd took command of this new acquisition and put her immediately to sail, and ironically took the Captain of the vessel along with them just for the rough ride; the Quedagh Merchant herself was a four hundred ton ship and highly capable of ramming any vessel or could out-speed any current design of naval vessel in her wake; she was the weapon of choice for the day. And Kidd, by his own volition, had already turned renegade having chanced this acquisition, and his duties and services to the King's Navy were all now but gone and swiftly becoming a distant memory. The life of pomp and ceremony was behind him and a newly found Privateer's life was on the cards for Captain William Kidd, and yet somehow he already knew this was going to be his very undoing. After upgrading the Quedagh Merchant to full battle configuration, she became a vessel fit to engage the Admiralty at any time.

CHAPTER ELEVEN

'The Seventh lamp'

Hastings sat down next to the large empty book cabinet and placed his leather-clad feet upon the wooden sea chest with a very distinctive heavy thud, then took a rather long deep breath as he gazed around the chamber, taking in its various nooks and crannies, then puckered his lips whilst still reeling and the buzzing from the rum which had somehow relieved him of his short term senses. He smiled inwards and smirked to himself in a smug but comfortable manner then threw his hat across the room and smiled nonchalantly as it landed cleanly square on the table top. In an effort to congratulate himself for such good shooting practice, he leaned backwards and bumped his head on something solid. 'Ouch oh, arrgh, bloody thing.' He turned quickly and stared at a large item that had been covered with a large piece of cotton sail. He lifted one end of the sheet then just fell into absolute silence and bewilderment as he gazed upon what he thought was a large jacket stand, but it was really too short in height, *maybe it was for very small people* he thought, then started laughing again. As he undraped the sail sheet from the structure, he observed an object that should have really been lighting up the back end of the small cabin as opposed to being inert, as he realised it was still a nice candle stick with seven branches. Although his bunk was not of the usual dimensional shape and size for the normal crew, Hastings made no complaint as he had dwelled in far worse, albeit it was a good enough in size for now and although the space had been used more often as a spare store room and was literally kept in darkness as Kidd had ensured that this was kept very dark and locked to ensure none of the crew decided to take the candlestick for a walk ashore and was swapped for a lady of the night or a few ales. But Kidd had permitted him to choose any cabin as long as it was near to the ward room. Of course, by default, this cabin was the nearest and had been the quarters of the previous ship's surgeon who had been found dead having been allegedly poisoned, if rumours were to be believed.

The other part of this particular story goes along the lines of: that was since this unfortunate incident had occurred, which states that the ship had been boarded by unknown visitors during the night and simply murdered the surgeon. And as a direct result, the cabin had been blocked off using a makeshift bulkhead, which had just been literally re-opened prior to the arrival of Hastings, ordered open by the Captain. It was unlikely that any of the crew had been given a chance to search the dwellings or take time to clean out the bunk either and the captain had kept it under lock and key until now. Hastings was very much amused. 'Wow!' he exclaimed softly. 'Now that's a pretty dandy candlestick, even if I say so myself. It's a pretty large light holder indeed, so where in hell's coffers did you come out from?' he muttered whilst beginning to pull himself into the upright position in order to view the seven branches of the substantial candle holder in greater detail the proviso of having a one-to-one discussion with the lighting implement. Only three small wax candles had been placed in the smaller holders on the table top and they each flickered whilst struggling to light up the space. Hastings reached over and gave the stand a quick ping with his finger. It appeared somewhat solid and was very sturdy. He quizzed the fine lattice work around the stem and the ornate base and was quite amused as to how the menorah had been physically constructed; to him, it looked like one piece of metal. The young midshipman had obviously at some point lit the candles before anticipating that the officer was returning to his bunk after a few ales with the master of the vessel and had disappeared on decks.

Hastings took a sniff of the night dry salt air and then froze as he spied several Aramaic or alchemic (Egyptian) inscriptions and strange lettering that had been engraved across the small panels of each cup or candle holder. The menorah candlestick was certainly made of a heavy substance but no way was this size of an old lighting appliance ever going to be made from pure solid gold as it would literally cost thousands upon thousands of pieces of eight, and if one would even want to purchase such an item today, especially in this modern age of 1696, it was certainly a lifetime salary one hundred fold in cost.

The Buccaneer and newly appointed side kick of Captain William Kidd wiped his chin again and slouched down slightly before abruptly standing up, and whilst placing both hands around the neck of the candelabra, he began trying to shake it but soon realised that this was not a run of the mill candlestick but something very significant indeed, apart from being rather heavy. And on the off chance of acquiring the piece, Hastings was one who would certainly have liked to own such an elegant piece for his home, but Kidd would have his guts for garter bands if he even tried to move or even hint at taking it. Hastings sat down and quietly fell into a drunken stupor as the outside world came alive and as the day crew were on top decks finding the morning light. The gunners and carpenters met the new day head on and Hastings awoke a short while later. He thought that before doing anything else he opened up his little red private diary notebook and made a few very important notes, writing down the following points of interest which he had taken from recent exposure to some rather interesting documents, and took another peek at the large gold Menorah. 'Shit, it was real,' he exclaimed quietly to himself, thinking it was this the relic that the Holy Order was searching for. Was it a relic stolen by the British then acquired by a pirate and then acquired by another pirate? Hastings reached for his notebook from within his jacket pocket and started scribbling notes in his best handwriting. Firstly, the words Insual Rohor. The distance of 2810 miles (nautical) from London to Oak Island. The last letters of the DM Code – the UOU 45 degrees, the union of theory...do the D = 500 and the M = 1000 and union is 150.

He then stopped writing and asked himself another question. 'Yes, but fifteen hundred bloody what miles or feet?' Then he continued scribbling again. 'Topographical location of Oak Island, Honey Bay - Chester Nova Scotia, Rose bay, or the cove; are these numbers of all the mean coordinates? - 44 54628 - 64 241753.' He then leaned over the chest and picked up a rather sad-looking version of a very well-used bible, but in doing so, the hardcover simply tore and fell away from the spine and sent a few pages of the book cascading down on to the floor below. 'Shit.' He tutted for a moment and began clearing the loose pages up when he came across a single small piece of beige coloured vellum amongst the papers which had been cleverly tucked within the last two or three pages of the 1600's KJV-King James Version and best-selling book of the day - the bible. He laid the good book down on the wooden sea chest and began reading the vellum page on its own, only finding to his surprise that he had stumbled across some quite interesting details on the construction and design of the very 'candle holder' that he had just been quizzing earlier in his semi-drunken stupor. Then he recognised the piece behind him from the rough drawing on the page; he then took time to read the detail – The Menorah of King Solomon. In order to make a lampstand of pure gold, the hammersmith must first hammer out its base and shaft. Kemp Hastings toyed with his glasses whilst squinting his eyes for better vision and straightened them up on the bridge of his nose before taking a very long, drawn-out look at the menorah in the cabin behind him again, then concentrated on the interesting text. 'Oh, my heaven and Lord, have we been really so gifted as to become the custodian of such an ancient and important item? But what about Kidd? Surely, the pirate would want to sell it for the gold and the many trappings of the good life, or perhaps this was the Lord's test of religious loyalty?'

He read the parchment whilst running his finger through every line in the text: 'Then make the flowerlike cups, buds, and blossoms of the one piece with them. Six branches are to extend from the side of the lampstand – three on one side and three on the other branch – balanced in design, three cups shaped like almond flowers with buds and blossoms which are to be placed on each branch, and three on the next branch, and the same for all six branches extending from the lampstand. And on the lamp stand, there are to be four cups shaped like almond flowers with buds and blossoms, one bud shall be under the first pair of branches extending from the lamp stand, a second bud under the second pair, and a third bud under the third pair – six branches in all. The buds and branches shall be all of one piece with the lampstand, and each hammered out of pure gold. Then make seven lamps - and set them on it so that they light the space in front of it. Its wick trimmers and trays are of pure gold, a talent of pure gold is also to be used for the lampstand and all these accessories. See that you make them according to the pattern shown to you on the mountain.' Kemp Hastings simply shuddered with fear and froze as he read the words 'on the mountain'. He knew parts of the bible story or at least he thought he did, and he had always thought that Moses and the other biblical characters had never really been prolific in his own understanding of the bible story, and now, right there and then, he was literally going to be haunted by them; he was very suddenly caught up in something that could become one of the deepest and most religious of things in his life, and beginning with spurious origins that even he could not explain.

If this item was a real deal and the parchment was authentic and correct, and this was what he thought the article of faith really was, then he also knew that he was now part of very important biblical history and his life would also be in jeopardy.

His thoughts were stemming back to just a few weeks prior when he recalled a conversation with William Kidd when the stone of destiny was a point of conversation and Kidd had quite literally dismissed or passed off the subject as being mere hearsay at the time stating that it was indeed just conjecture and humorous chit chat, and should not to be discussed any further on board his vessel. Those were the Captain's exact words and orders and he wanted them obeyed. His answer was along the lines of, 'And who would want to buy a chunk of big black and purple rock that was a pillow, anyway?' If a greater understanding of history had been known by the sea Captain, then this is where he would have also have known that the Holy Menorah of King Solomon and the Davidic Line had once stood proudly on top of the 'Stone of Destiny' or Jacob's Pillow' within the temple of Solomon. And this story would have been certainly inextricably mixed with other great tales of riches, deception, and commerce as to how things came into the Western society. It was commercial goods like tea, cannabis plants, and other social drugs, coupled with religious artefacts that also came into social being or had found their way into general discussion. But at this juncture kept alive by secret societies and thanks be to those ancient Knights crusaders who exploited the use of their practical human talents and resources and was an important lesson was learned from the many scryers and knights who sampled not only hashish, but through ingesting Isma'ilis, or other interesting hallucinogenic fauna and flora whilst they were introduced 'an escape' into the modern world.

The other world of free and open trade was becoming a multi-faceted market indeed and sadly the marketing of holy relics and church silver and gold ware was very much a lucrative business and were on the increase. Modern day alchemists and scientists were forever on the look-out for cheap gold and silver trinkets, and by the late 17th century, it was possible to buy almost every commodity, including human beings, as people trafficking was becoming the new fad. And it was a trait and trade that was raping South America, Africa, and the West Indies like wildfire, but sadly, life was very cheap. People trafficking was a trait that the Knights Templar frowned upon and they would shut down any trading of souls very rapidly by way of the sword and would act as quickly as they should as the need arose.

Hastings had considered other notions at this time and pondered more on the free trade of such nice things as silks, drugs, and on some occasions technical or astronomical equipment because in those older days he knew that cannabis was just a confection as was Turkish delight was a luxury, and he knew that many people could not afford to buy such items. But, if Kidd was working the old ways in the maritime sense, then his cargo was local hemp, he would provide a ship with tons upon tons of the stuff and fuelled a market that used hemp for making, things like ships ropes and flax linen and animal hide for industrial purposes, and let us not to forget the many uses of coconuts as they were becoming the best highly sought after commodity or article in great demand from the world market, especially as they provided both food and nutrients coupled with a hard surface shell and large leaves, all of which were found in one plantation, all items that he would eventually have to take with him to Nova Scotia, and liaise and trade with the Miq Maqs Indian colony who craved such foreign objects, and who were a small colony living on the outer edges of what is known today as New Scotland or Nova Scotia. Hastings recalled the hero of the day a man called 'Glooslap' and he may have been a generic Indian and was a very active Templar in his time. The Officer Kemp Hastings had been lucky enough to have been involved in an earlier journey to old Canada when he was employed as a young sailor and had found himself caught up in many religious teachings and was simply too young to understand any of it, but he listened none the less, albeit as a young man he was not so worldly wise as the old skipper was, but he learned, and the Captain would often say, 'the man above will look after you' as he attempted a bit of father figure support for his young crew.

Hastings at the time had very little inclination nor the drive in his soul to chase God or religion; the sea and the open vast expanses of the waters were his heaven and at the end of the aquatic working day, the legend and ancient figure of Poseidon would see him on his deliverance, and Poseidon would take him on a path that may lead to nowhere, but Glooslap, on the other hand, was known for his pragmatism and vision and was instrumental in bringing certain new-age theories into the Indian culture and indeed the outside world. He had demonstrated the use of fishing with nets and making or weaving clothing from what would have been known as hemp or flax today. Hastings stopped thinking for a few seconds and began reading the many glyphs and symbols across the interesting candlestick and stared intently at the Menorah for quite some time. He also took time to ask himself a few searching biblical questions. Could this really be the holy relic from King Solomon's temple of the ancient world? Could it be that by some stroke of luck or fate that he now had to contemplate preserving this article of great religious faith as opposed to just selling it on just for profit? Perhaps, Kidd had already thought about that, and or the first time in his life, Hastings was mentally and utterly 'buggered'. Just then the door to his cabin slowly opened and the Officer looked up. Suddenly, towering over him were the two biggest tattooed sailors he had ever encountered; the expression on his face must have said it all, and yet he sparked into the façade and persona of his old previous hardened British Naval Officer act. 'Don't you bloody knock before you enter the cabin of a merchant officer? Don't you know that respect has to be earned by not only the officers but also by the ship's crew? You!' he said pointing at the Gunners mate Edward Townsend. 'You should know only too well that when the Captain is sleeping or indisposed, I take command of the vessel, and responsibility for the crew, now what the hell do you two want anyway?' He demanded as he viewed the two men yet again with greater interest. Both men stood at over six foot and five inches in height and were both broad enough not to fit within the large door frame, especially whilst standing together in their well-trodden and very much travelled leather boots, but these two gorillas were certainly not the pair of chaps one would wish to encounter in the dark or encounter in the very dangerous alleyways of old world Madagascar, unless, of course, if you were looking for trouble and that they were both on your side. The first of these butt ugly sea-gunners was the educated ships gunner's mate and appeared to be a man or at best guess a beast, whichever suited one's outlook, and was of a fresh skin complexion supporting a unique crop of very short white hair which stuck upwards like a single fiery flame on the top of his head, and was simply tattooed from head to arse with several depictions of bows and arrows coupled with little matchstick men appearing as ink drawings interspersed all across his body. This hardened and battle experienced sailor had served several years on Royal Naval frigates during the peninsula wars whilst fighting the French and Dutch and was certainly by any description a seasoned salty mariner; however, his partner in whatever crime one could think of, and I am only guessing here when I say that there could be a certain list of criminal activity that may well be as long as his twenty-year service record of close detention, and stating that perhaps this character was not a model sailor by a long chalk. But by all accounts, he was still as loyal as a dog to any skipper who would furnish him with ale and food. And Captain Kidd, of course, was the 'feeder'.

Kidd would call these men the spinal column or proverbial backbone of the modern 17th century merchant shipping world, and these were men who were certainly feared by most other maritime nations. Ships from many countries would quite literally evade any confrontation if they even suspected or held any inclination that a Buccaneer Vessel they were about to attack held three or four of the East India Company's elite henchmen within their ranks and would consider contingency tactics. Hastings then pointed to the Gunners mate. 'You there, Mister Townsend, tell me, please, why the hell do you have a shit load of little Indian arrows tattooed across your body? Tell me, sir, why would you want to do that?' The Gunners mate shuffled in his stance and smiled before responding to the question, 'Kidd did it, sir, he paid me forty pieces of eight to carry his private secret with me at all times, so after a few nights on the old Pussers rum and ale, I ended up with the symbols of an Indian nation strategically inked across my body.'

Hastings was almost gobsmacked then quizzed further, 'So, you are saying that you got those tattoos because the Captain asked you to carry his secret? What secret is that then?' he asked as he stood up and gazed across the large arms of the very large man. In doing so he attempted to raise the side of the sailor's shirt to follow the line of tiny arrows that led up to the man's left armpit, when the physical and muscular mass of the attending naval 'Orangutan' or Gunner's mate number two slowly leaned forward and picked up the Officer by the shoulders and moved him away to one side from his sea-mate. 'Cannot let you do that either, sir. Captain's direct orders. You see the Captain also paid me very handsomely to ensure that no one spied over 'Brass's' back.'

The Officer placed his hands in his trouser pockets and turned toward the Menorah and gave out a huge puff of air, then turned again. Thinking that the candlestick would certainly be very heavy and would not be easy to move, and maybe he had just identified a couple of ill-educated but very strong mules to aid such a task. The Officer tweaked his own nose and spoke out loudly, 'Brass's what!' Hastings turned slightly and gazed directly at the two sailors again. 'Monkey's came the quick reply. His nickname, sir... it's short for Brass Monkey, Gunner's matey here,' he said pointing at his colleague who was now staring upwards at the deck head. 'This Gunner here, sir, he once fed eighteen guns with sixteen brass monkey gun-shot confetti within three minutes during the battle of 'Honey Island' where three frigates belonging to the French were totally destroyed, and this 'man-monkey' here was totally responsible.' The Officer nodded in acknowledgement and smiled again. 'Natural hero then, Mister Townsend, but don't think for one minute that muscle power alone wins the day, but for your efforts, I must agree they are very well deserved and do sound very interesting indeed, and worthy of further discussion. You! What's your name if you do indeed have one?' asked the Officer in an almost flippant tone and waited patiently for an answer. 'Me, sir, I am called Jeff, although I am actually born Mid-shipman Richards, the crew all call me 'Grapeshot' due to the way I always ram the shipyard confetti down the barrels of the Guns with my heavy baton to ensure that Brass's cannon delivers an impact so powerful that it will rip a man's head off at the shoulders from over one hundred feet away, just like eating and spitting grapes, sir. You see, we never 'fail' do me and Brassy, we are unique and we work together as a team.'

The Officer shook his head in almost disbelief before he spoke, 'So, you think you were born a mid-shipman? Well, that's very odd, Mister Jeff, and also very important to know, so, okay then... so tell me, Mister Townsend and Mister Jeff the Grapeshot, what do you want?' The two men looked at each other, nodded, then left the chamber closing the door very gently behind them, and had departed without saying a word. Hastings stood in total awe and waited. 'What a couple of ruddy and very strange men,' he said softly to himself and slowly stroked the gold cross member of the Menorah whilst muttering away to himself, 'Well, you are certainly going to be safe with those two gentlemen around.'

CHAPTER TWELVE

'The Cockpit'

As the night drew in, the crew had taken their food for the day and were making ready for the night routine, down in the cockpit on the vessel a place where most of the crew would assemble to take time to relax and quite often the older sea dogs would recite tales of the high seas exploits and relive intrepid adventures, which often ended in death, destruction, or catastrophe, or they would allude to great riches being discovered across the known world. But, in essence, this was the social world of the mariner, and the 'art' of telling tall or exaggerated stories was an embedded gift and deemed an important part of ships rituals. The Officer sat down on the round half barrel and listened intently as the ships cook and chief bottle washer 'Tee Chow' started to recite a tale about a man and a map, and what was to become a journey leading to the discovery of a huge wealth of gold and silver. Tee Chow crouched down and walked amongst the men acting like a hunch back stalking the market streets. 'It was 15th April in the year 1670 something', when the ghost ship the 'The Flying Dutchman' was first sighted just two miles off the coast of Newfoundland and it was said by the fishermen that she was drifting silently and no one was at the helm; it was also said that she had a strange red glow over her decks; it was a bloody red shine possessed by the devil himself. But, a few days later, the vessel was found still drifting silent and very cold looking when the ship was eventually boarded by some 'sea whalers' from the eastern provinces. They had discovered a horrific and deadly scene that was set before them. The Captain said it was as if the devil himself had visited three of the ship's crew and had slaughtered them without mercy. The three men were found still hanging across the broken large yard arm, each man covered in his own blood from head to toe, and infested with roaches and flies each sailor completely covered in brown and white crow shit, but the very strange thing about this crew was that they had all been relieved of their skin, their flesh had been ripped off in slices having been cut from their backs and shoulders, strip by strip in some cases. They say it had been sliced off in such a way that each strip as long as the yard arm been torn from their bodies with a precision of a surgeon, as if to keep the skin intact, long rectangular strips. Now, this was no ordinary hanging or high-end flogging either, this was horrific ritual torture and a very deliberate killing. It was rumoured that these three men held such a secret that collectively they had knowledge of the ancients and they had all died for the secrets they kept.'

Kemp Hastings sat at the back of the cockpit space and listened with great interest as the story was being delivered with passion and fierce delivery by Tee Chow who was loving every moment as he recited his best ghost story ever. He watched with even more interest as the assembled crew members were almost fixed on Tee Chow as they listened to the cook's very tall tale. The cook winked at Hastings and continued in his story. 'Now I hear that one of the escaping crew had witnessed this horrible torture event, and had managed to hide himself deep inside the foc'sle cavity amongst the dead fish and old ropes during this horrible raid, and after the raiding party had plundered the ship and had gone. The salty sailor eventually escaped from the 'ship' and was found lurking in an ale house under great mental disarray and was busily drinking himself to certain death due to what he had witnessed. Now, listen to me carefully, the description of these raiders was such that they wore long purple robes and had embroidered patches of golden dragons and lions, they held weapons that sent pillars of fire high into the skies and yet they never spoke a single word throughout the encounter. But it was reported that they had red eyes that shone beams of hatred into any man's soul who dared gaze upon their faces.

However, somehow, they knew what each other was thinking, but you must remember this my mateys you should also know and understand that the marine vessel, the 'The Dutchman', was no ordinary vessel either; she was driven by the devil's four horsemen of the apocalypse and even today I am told that Davey Jones fears this fierce entity, and although the ship was a fast smaller square-rigged vessel with only 12 small cannon to her name for protection, she was only vulnerable whilst at bay, but her strength was in her feisty crew and her agility to negotiate the shallow waters of Honey Bay – Insula Roher in and around the waters of Arcadia. But as she sat under anchor in the very shallow waters, she was boarded in the dead of night by this crew of Devil warriors. Rumour has it that each of the three crew men held a secret symbol of knowledge in the shape of a tattoo that had been etched into their skin and collectively held the secret to this forbidden knowledge. Now each man had a figure of a man and one had a woman and they were standing in a graveyard that was said to house the grave of Jesus, and that's the great secret. And remember that each man had been found hung and their skin flailed and left to the crows for the deathly secret they kept. This was a deadly pact with the devil and the price was their souls being the penalty for failure. But let me tell you this, they held not only a symbol of hatred but also a map; it was a map made in four pieces and each piece had also been tattooed into the skin of these skilled sailors.'

As the tension in the room grew warmer and higher, Hastings recalled that back then Kidd had been angered by something and had indeed kicked open the main door which suddenly burst open and the skipper had entered and drew his pistol. Hastings also recalled his comments. 'Bed time, lads. I cannot have you listening to these 'horrible' tales when you have work to do in the morning. Sleep, yes, sleep that is what you need, not being made scared half shitless by some old seadog tales. Now, get yer heads down and think about the sexy women in Madagascar and the life we are going to lead once we set sail from this hell hole.' Hastings stood up and stepped forward. He remembered thinking that the Captain spoke a few soft and very well-chosen words. 'You should not be so foolish to believe all these tales you hear, Mister Hastings, these stories have tails as long as the coastline of Scotland and beyond if you listen hard enough.' Hastings then pulled the door shut and responded, 'Well, I certainly won't be looking for the devil's tail tonight if that's what you mean.'

Kidd had also stopped in his tracks and turned swiftly. Hastings shuffled forward as he moved a little closer and was close enough to also recall the smell of his ale stained breath as the Skipper took another deep breath that was followed by a deathly gaze of the man, and he seemed to have stopped moving. 'Oh no, Mister Hastings, Tee Chow is not reciting some concocted story to appease the crew. He was telling a true story of an event that actually happened; that night on the Avon was hell in motion fourteen men disappeared and only three were found on the yard arm, but those poor tortured souls were not the targets of this secret society. These invaders were an ancient order of Knights who swore to take revenge on the buccaneers who stole their cargoes and gold, and let me tell you this, my friend, if they find the crew that dared to attack their ships, then hell will not be far enough away to hide.'

The Captain then very suddenly cut short his story. 'We will talk later, but for now, I must sober up.' These were probably the last sentiments or serious words that Hastings had heard from the skipper directly before all the antics in New York had occurred and before Kidd was hauled away under the kosh to face trial. Taking no chances, the Adventure Prize had slipped her moorings and was off to better climes.

CHAPTER THIRTEEN

'The Business end of Piracy'

The East India Company – three years earlier.

Captain Kidd had faced his first officer and explained the setup of the Shipping traffic, which included the important vessels of the East India Company, each vessel often sailing with their huge cargo holds filled for the taking. By the year 1679, when the captain of the Marine Vessel Halsewell was writing the first of his log book entries, which included his strategic sailing plans, the East India Company at the time was the single largest player in the global trading market. It should be noted that documents retained in the British Library's India Office collection reveal that a newly affluent class was emerging; it was deemed a company with drive and was instilled with an enthusiasm for imported goods such as cotton, silks, porcelain, tea, and spices, all of which were very valuable commodities in the emerging markets across not only Europe but also into the Americas. Kidd scratched the nape of his neck and once again took several moments whilst quizzing his audience of one. Meanwhile, Kemp Hastings listened intently and was quietly absorbing the potential future cargoes that could provide a very healthy future indeed. Early in his tenure as Lieutenant, Kidd had sailed with Captain for a short time as the guest of the East India Company, but the entire voyage was riddled and plagued with an almost hatred between the two as Kidd's interpretation of good seamanship was being personally pitched against this so-called seasoned Merchant Captain, an attitude on Kidd's part which really differed greatly between the two. The ten-month voyage to Calcutta, Bombay, finishing in Madras, was followed by an unscheduled onward voyage to Canton to pick up a load consisting of tea and porcelain which was another potentially very lucrative outlet for the Company. But it was also a very dangerous voyage as it cut through the pirate territory. Not only the pirates to evade but also the treacherous tides and the difficult waters to negotiate; there were, of course, the winds, waves, and the foul winter weather of the English Channel to consider, which also brought into question the shocking news about the widely reported wreck of the marine vessel the Halsewell which floundered just off the Dorset coast in the year 1686. A voyage that Kidd hailed as a certain event waiting to happen at the hands of the inept skipper, although Kidd himself had somehow managed to jump ship somewhere in and around the Straits of Gibraltar prior to the vessel crossing the channel. An account by two of the ship's officers who survived the shipwreck wrote a poem about the tragic loss of the captain and sadly his daughters and had included descriptions of a dramatic reconstruction of a shipwreck that caused a sensation in London, providing a further flavour of the public's appetite for information and sensationalism. This notion once dissipated as the stories and tales started to take adventurous shape once the media heard about the swashbuckling stories of piracy on the high seas. For centuries thereafter, tales and sagas and stories regarding smugglers and their smuggled goods provided a cheap alternative to the more expensive imports but also made good reading, but Kidd was wise and he quickly smelled a rat, but he also sniffed a golden window of great opportunity. However, in his mind, not much had changed in that respect of being a Pirate or Privateer for that matter up into the 18th and 19th centuries as commercial greed and tax evasion was as rife today as it was in the preceding two centuries. Albeit high taxes on imported goods were nearing 15% imposed by the British Government and made many luxury goods very expensive indeed, yet still highly desirable, any pirate can tell you that...

But illegally smuggled goods provided a quick solution to the actual problem. Alcohol, especially Brandy or smoking tobacco, and, of course, scented tea, which proved to be very popular consumer goods. And it was during this lucrative time the British Parliament passed another Act against smuggling. Captain Kidd started to slap a piece of vellum across the table top and began to vent his anger. 'These land lubbing, seat polishing, greedy bastards are strangling me every day with their unrelenting demand for more controls and more stupid taxes and more restrictive laws. Do these people not understand that in order for me to do their dirty work for them they have to let me breath normal air. Are these people mad! Kidd was obviously very annoyed and was simply venting his anger. At this juncture, Hastings stood up and left the small room, as it was times like this that the Captain would instantly erupt like a volcano and simply go right off the rails. Unfortunately for the galley rat and his man at arms, they had both entered the small cabin just as the Captain threw a pot of ale at the wooden desk and watched as it splashed over the single legal document sitting nearby, sending the sweet aroma of ale and bits of broken bread across the table top. He turned and spied the two men standing in front of him, each man witnessing the rage in the Captain's eyes, and they both froze in fear, each man waiting to be chastised for disturbing the Skipper in his moment of enraged anger, and they knew that an invite to hell might just be heading their way. The Captain took a very deep breath and nodded several times before standing up and grabbed his hat. He turned and faced his crew, then spoke softly, 'Not your concern, gentlemen. This is not your concern, not your bother, 'Tee Chow', and not your burden, Mister 'Raddy Anka. Thank you. Please leave me be for now,' he said waving both men to leave him alone. The two men, whilst grabbing their tunics with both hands, pulled across their chest buttons and began walking swiftly backwards in great haste, each of them trying to swiftly negotiate the narrow doorway just in case Kidd had taken a moment's leave of his senses and changed his mind.

As the door closed gently, Captain Kidd could hear them muttering to one another as they walked down the long corridor. 'What s'pose is eating the old man?' offered the galley rat Tea Chow to his colleague who was taking no chances of hearing the Cap'n calling them to get back and quickened his pace. 'No idea, but it's going to be very serious if the Cap'n has not left a mark on a living man in his fit of anger. Maybe he is getting older.' Tea Chow smiled a huge Philipino smile…Werr we got no 'probrems den, Capitano reave us arone, that's bruddy good.' Raddy Anka looked somewhat bemused and patted the cook on the back. 'Well, we had better be very careful because nothing good ever comes out of a situation where the Skipper is quiet. We best grab Brassy and Grapeshot and see what they think.' Meanwhile, the Captain held a parchment that depicted the logo of the East India Company in his fist. In the early days, he personally had targeted a few ships that he knew were hauling expensive cargoes and he quizzed the list in his hand and smirked as he acknowledged a few names of vessels that had been recorded by name and year of either their loss or their demise.

Ship:

- Adventure 1687 – Captain William Goodlad lost near Madras
- Advice 1700 Captain William Redhead Frigate lost near Fort St George

Kidd had logged some notes next to this list of marine details.

- Act of Parliament Pyrats
- Act of Parliament Duty of 15% taxes on goods.
- Anna 1700 – Lost from India, encountered the Avon Ascoti.. intercepted
- Anne 1660 – Captain Robert Knox – Captured Sinhalse
- Anne 1689 -Captain William Freke - supposedly wrecked at Madagascar, intercepted by the Adventure Galley or the Avon Ascoti under Shivaji's Forces.
- Anne Royal - 1620 – Captain Andrew Shilling – lost between London & Gravesend.
- Antelope – 1673 Captain John Goldsborough Captured by the Dutch
- Bantam -1671 lost at sea Captain William Barker
- Bawden – 1687 Attacked at Sai Tiago Bombay then seized Madagascar nr Massalege

As Kidd ran his finger down the list, he highlighted the known campaigns he had either been directly involved with or had supplied the maps that would eventually lead the Pirate charge against the East India Company for their treatment of him and his crew; however, Kidd showed no remorse as he acknowledged the fact that he had in reality plundered over £540,000 from the company over the last six years, and he had deliberately targeted the older EIC Voyages under which he had suffered a fair share of dangerous encounters, including the British Navy, but he had not bargained on being shadowed by the infamous vessel, the Avon Ascoti. Kidd had a gut instinct that he had encountered the vessel before as she had an odd-shaped extra rigging style that was difficult to forget, and he was sure hell-bent on finding out why this unruly ship had been raping the high seas whilst boasting the colours of the British Navy. The problem was that the British were sanctioning murder under the auspice that **'Dead men tell no tales',** hence, no survivors.

The list of Ships' names on the roll was quite comprehensive; the EIC had a vast fleet of over six hundred ships at this stage. He read on:

- The Bear 1619, Bee 1619, Bengal Merchant 1693, Berkley Castle 1694, Bombay Frigate 1700 (Attacked by Pirates 1707 Savaji sunk). Bonito 1655, Wrecked Madras, Canterbury 1703/4, Chambers Frigate 1709, Charles 1633 Destroyed by Fire, Claw 1685, Comfort 1638 attacked by Pirates Malabar sunk. Concord 1616, Crown 1671, Lost Taiwan, Defence 1623, captured by the Dutch.
- Defence 1695 Decoy Vessel used to destroy ships at sea. Degrave - beached Madagascar – *reassigned Avon Ascoti.*

William Kidd took a very deep breath and read the last few pages of the vellum again, he had just discovered that the EIC, the East India Company, had actually reassigned a beached vessel called the Degrave and renamed it the 'Avon Ascoti'. Was this in order to attack Pirate vessels at sea with impunity? The only flaw now being that Kidd was of the notion that he was simply dealing with a real physical vessel and not some Devil-driven myth or legend vessel that was designed to strike terror and fear into the hearts of the good old jolly jacktar Pirate. The old 700 Ton vessel would have carried at least 52 Guns and was a certain challenge if caught in face to face in direct battle and would have been a worthy adversary to encounter. She was also last known to have been under the command of one Captain John Benbow and a Captain Young, and although she had run aground and was stuck fast at some point in her life, she was eventually freed up and sailed an intrepid journey, making it as far as the island of Mauritius. The story goes that the crew eventually 'Kidnapped' the black King of the island, and after an intrepid gun fight lasting more than six hours, the crew had fled and made it off the island. Kidd gave out a loud laugh and wiped his brow with his red handkerchief before delving into his satchel and produced another bottle of fine Pussers rum. 'Well, those landlubbers won't catch me with this deceptive plan, bloody amateurs.' Kidd gazed over the parchment again trying to work out how many vessels had actually been attacked by Pirates in the last twelve months knowing that he himself was responsible for seven recorded encounters and had survived a couple of attacks of which he fought back and acquired their cargo and the Armenian ships, which were designated as spoils of high seas war and ran those vessels for some time.

That was, of course, until the involvement of the East India Company who were engaged by the High Commission in London to investigate Captain Kidd for his out of scope pirate activities, which was not in line with his letter of marque, and who had some rather powerful political friends in very high places.

Actual Vessels - Attacked by Pirates:

- Jewel 1641 Pirate John Mucknell, Lion 1625 attacked
- Little James 1627 & Little Josiah attacked by Pirates, *Mocha Frigate* – Renamed *'Resolution'* Four Pirate crew hanged at execution dock wapping.
  (The true story of Captain William Kidd – The Pirate Hunter by Richard Zacks).
- Moon 1625 attacked Dutch pirates
- Morning Star 1669 - Pirates
- Prosperous 1702 – Pirates, Royal Charles – Dutch Pirates,
- Samuel Incident 1692 – French Pirates
- Scout 1625 Arab Pirates
- Star 1619 Pirates Dutch, Susannah 1705 Pirates Dutch

- Albemarle 1708 - Ethiopia crew left to die at the hands of the natives.
- Anson 1747 – Pirates of Malabar Bombay.
- Unicorn - scuttled by an explosion by Captain Webb to hide the vessel and murdering six of his own crew.

Reference:

- Juan Esteban Ubilla – The Horsehoe Expedition.
- The 'DM' Code Lat & Long

CHAPTER FOURTEEN

'Inkychung - Madagascar'

Three very drunken sailors sat and chatted about wine, wimmen, and song whilst congregated around a large oak table that was littered with empty beer jugs and what appeared to be the remnants of someone's half-eaten chicken dinner. The taller and most muscular of the trio had just finished his three-hour session of sitting quietly with the infamous Malaysian tattooist, Inkychung, a man whose reputation across the middle east was synonymous with excellence created by his talents and perhaps mainly due to his ability to create great godly artwork in the form of the masters of the ancient art, and perhaps also because Inkychung had created tattoos for perhaps one of the most infamous sailors of all time that had traversed the open seas. His most famous client being Captain Henry Morgan privateer and all-round nasty bastard who had commissioned to have three small diamonds tattooed not only on each of his ears but had two large religious crosses 'inked' on to each one of his buttock cheeks. The Adventure Galley crew, however, were not yet as famous or feared as Henry Morgan's crew were, but their very own Captain William Kidd was beginning to gain quite a reputation that reflected some of his more abusive antics, which were becoming a legend in his own lifetime, and no matter what location the vessel was docked at, there was always some sort of challenge to the reputation that

'Kidd' the slaughterer had tortured one of his crewmembers during the trip, and that his excuse was usually for reasons around high treason to the crown. Or, the other common reason was that these were sailors who had literally challenged the Skipper for control of his vessel. The current rumour in circulation being centred in and around the small island was that Kidd had pulled out his two muskets and shot four of his crew for insubordination, but, of course, a fact Kidd greatly refuted and rejected this claim because he always stated that he only has two muskets and each one only carried one shot of ball each. 'My goodness, Bosun, these rumours are getting out of control. They will be saying that I was fighting single-handed with Davey Jones and the King of Jamaica next.' Gary Bertie, the Adventurer's longest-lasting crew member, and Bosun smiled and ordered four large jugs of ale and then set them down on the table in front of the Skipper then spoke. 'Well, Cap'n Inkychung will have finished the boys by now, Skipper. We will have to be careful as they will have painful backs and probably the most valuable skin in the history of Tattoos to care for,' the Captain picked up a single jug of ale and smirked as he spoke into his mug of ale. 'Well, Bosun, if we don't protect them very well, then I will have your porky hide made into a nice little handbag and your little pink cherub will be carried within it for the rest of eternity should you screw up, but now, my dear fellow, drink your ale and let's get on with our master plan together, but remember, I do agree with you that we cannot afford for anyone to spy those tats; we will take no chances, so make sure Brassy and Grapeshot take care of them, but you are quite right, we need to keep a close on the crew as well.'

CHAPTER FIFTEEN

'Guests of Dishonour'

If the meeting with the ship's crew in the cockpit several weeks back was not bad enough to shiver ye'r timbers, especially as the crew had spun many ancient mariner tales of death, woe, struggle, and war. Each account conveyed to highlight the mysterious life at sea and encounters with ancient sea monsters, blood eating vampire bats, and killer sea snakes that were attacking ships unannounced, which in themselves should have sent shivers of doubt and fear running up and down the spine, then Hastings was certainly about to have another encounter and very rude awakening. And that was when he was confronted by two jolly moronic Jacktar sailors who had stumbled into the confides of 'One Eyed Jacks' on the island, and incidentally, one of the most infamous pirates watering holes near to the sea inlet of 'Holly Cove' and who were on their own run little ashore for a general good old time. The tavern was aptly named as the term 'One Eyed Jacks' as this was, in essence, a person who shows the good side of their character while simultaneously hiding the other side of themselves, and who could be deemed incredibly repulsive, insincere, malicious, and untrustworthy, and could be mirrored against Dr. Jekyll and Mister Hyde as an example, but given this was Madagascar Scallywag 'Pirates' fit this particular bill. However, to the uneducated masses, it should be noted that Holly

Cove was also the last known location of a ship that was wrecked on the rocky outcrop in the early part of the 16th century in a violent storm, and it was rumoured that her Ghost ship has been seen to haunt the earie coastline of Southern Madagascar to this very day. The name of the ship was the infamous pirate vessel the 'Avon Ascoti', and only as recently as three months ago was she seen just sitting two miles or so just off the coast when seven members of the local population, whilst drinking, had witnessed a similar vessel coasting silently along in the distant mists with her masts and sails apparently alit with fingers of fire and was lighting up the moonlit night skies.

Hastings had just supped his final ale and was about to leave the table when the two Jacktar sailors sat down beside him and for no apparent reason grabbed him forcibly by the jacket lapels and demanded to know the whereabouts of the elusive Captain William Kidd. The Buccaneer remained calm and collective whilst he sat back down on the wooden bench and offered the two gentlemen to sit down and share a beer or three, and they could discuss their odd request. Hastings was first to speak: 'That's kind of odd because I was looking for Captain Kidd here myself. He told me that he would often come here and 'spend a night cracking jenny's tea cup' (Wine, wimmen, and merriment in a house of ill repute).' Hastings, knowing full well that Kidd was indeed dead, decided to stay and see what these morons had to offer. 'Although I had also heard he was dead, hung by the British Navy several weeks back for piracy and murder, but you know how rumours can be down here, but then again, I also heard that only last week he had dropped anchor somewhere down the coast and was looking for a new crew, and that was about five days ago.' As Hastings tried to relax a little more and quell the situation, he could smell the strong aroma from the black tar, which was splashed over the clothes and linen of the older gentleman, and was very much dominating the surrounding airspace; the pirate also spied a small tattoo of a small menorah candlestick on the man's left wrist and tried to engage his aggressors with a better line of attack. 'Not a common tattoo for a man to have. Unless you were part of a secret clan or group perhaps.' Hastings suddenly realised that this moron could actually hold part of the old DM Code affair that Anson had scribbled about in his earlier notes, as there was mention of men with tattoos on their hands. He waited quietly and patiently but not one of them offered a single response. Kemp tried his luck and started a different tack of conversation entirely.

'I can see from your wrist that you are from the 'House of Solomon, Knights Templar, Priory of Sion.' A certain brotherhood. My friend has a similar tattoo mark on his left breast, but I do not often get to meet fellow crusaders in those sort of places, especially men who are part of a secret group, especially ones so 'illuminated as your good selves obviously are. Mind you, I once did meet a man on an island called 'Le' Reunion', just over there somewhere, who had a tattoo of a cross on his back, but he was not a very bright man, but I do recall that he had the same tattoo on his chest the exact same as that one there on your hand. Huge it was, but I found out much later that he had another tattoo on his left shoulder of the same real seventh lamp symbol and he also had a map, I suppose you're...' The old man suddenly smiled with a grin that would sink a man at warship and Hastings immediately took the initiative to shut up as he spied that the man's front row of teeth were very uneven and resembled an old cemetery consisting of a set of gravestones that had been battered to pieces by the elements and had become rotten under the constant barrage of fire and brimstone for centuries from above. Albeit he could not help almost vomiting from the warm stench and aromatic smell of the man's actual stinking breath, it was much repugnant to say the very least. Hastings would say it was a mix of warm sea fish gut coupled with a dash of wild warthog shit and steeped in copious amounts of honey ale. The old man smiled a funny sort of grin then commented, 'Well, tattoos are a subject we will talk about later, but for now, my friend, we want your ship.' It was just then that the younger and uglier of the two men raised his hand and rammed a large wooden-handled Indian long-bladed curved cookery knife deep into the timbers of the table top and slowly leaned forward. Hastings was as equally taken aback as he was once again struck by another waft of offending fishy odour breath with the same damn offensive potency and smell as his brother in slime was. But this time it was emanating from a man who had no teeth at all, and he smirked boldly nonetheless and continued to stare back at him whilst nodding and tilting his head. The Buccaneer was thinking that his newly found death wielding smelly friends should have taken time to either have a bath or even suffer a shave or even both especially before going out and getting drunk on the town in such idyllic surroundings, and if Hastings was going to be brutally honest he would say that they were probably infested with other little bugs and beastie things as well, a host of exotic creatures and alien microbes. And just before the Buccaneer could swing his leg around the table and take off in haste much like the wind, he had already surmised knowing that things around the table were getting too close and too hot for comfort probably because he wanted to live quite a bit longer and he had already contemplated fleeing.

As he watched carefully as the toothless pirate of a man retracted the long blade from the oak plinth and began pointing it directly in his direction, mainly at his left eye, pointy end first, the uglier of the two gentlemen spoke: 'This little pointed baby has removed more than just eyes and ears in its lifetime, you know, but when this blade is held in these deadly killing hands and wielded in such places like this hellish hell hole of a cesspit, especially with me on this end then and you on the wrong end, I will command your very future. Now tell us where Captain Kidd is located and his little chink side kick that weasel of a man - Tee Chow, co's - we want to know where they are both hiding.' Just then a young lady approached the table. 'I will have no fighting and murderous activity in my bar; now drink up and go take your problems somewhere else, or I will set the dogs on you.' The one known as Naru spoke out, 'If you tell us now and we might let you live a little bit longer. You see we want to speak to them two nasty little people in a hurry. So, don't play games with us because we know who you are. We followed you here from the coast down by the Pirates lair and you never walked here to this island either, so 'it happens' you must have a ship sitting somewhere, so where are they and where is our ship?'

The older man then placed a hand over the handle of the knife and spoke softly, 'Steady, Naru, must keep calm, my friend, we can be reasonable. You see, my friend, I cannot really control him when he gets like this; he is just too uptight sort of like an animal in captivity, and perhaps one that needs to sow its oats, if you know what I mean, and Naru here seems to constantly fight his anxieties and demons as you can observe he is clearly frustrated in pain. But let me tell you this much, he has killed many men before today, and, yes, he has indeed scooped out many an eyeball has our swashbuckling hero.'

This was the ongoing account of Mister Manoj De Mhal the other pirate at arms whilst trying to scare Hastings into submission. 'So, you see, we want Kidd because he has our money and has stolen our ship as well and we want to claim it all back from him. So, I think you had probably better tell us where he is before we scoop out yer eyes, yer gizzards, and yer liver, and feed them to the big black birds over there.' Hastings took a deep breath and glanced at the large ravens that sat on the wooden fence waiting for a good 'tit bit' for lunch. Hastings then took a few moments to calm himself down and was just about to start a full-blown healthy fist fight when two great clumps of human flesh in the shape of two massive clenched fists came swiftly down from above and struck each of the Jacktars right on the middle of their heads. Hastings heard a funny sort of crumpling sound as the two scallywags just seemed to have frozen then blinked having been rendered instantly unconscious. Hastings uncontrollably let out a burst of very uncontained laughter. Both of the men sort of semi smiled as the remaining remnants of their infested teeth fell out of their mouths and found the hard shale below on the ground. The older man's head had flopped forward and struck the table. The other man was a different scenario completely, having received his healthy dunk on the top of the head. The sailor seemed to have just frozen on the spot and was out cold but oddly enough still sitting in the upright position. Hastings smiled another huge smile and burbled a gargled an incomprehensible comment, along the lines of: 'Just like the old times in Malagasy isle, I would say, gentlemen.'

The body and torso's that were attached to the bulk of the fists then picked up the two jolly Jack tars by the scruff of their jolly necks and threw them over their respective shoulders, then as a group headed for the confides of the brig on board the Adventure, which was docked no less than two miles away down the coast. Hastings walked beside the two giant Gunner sailors as they made their merry way down the mountain pathway that led to the sandy beach head and eventually led them on to a small wooden boat that lay in waiting. Hastings commented as he touched the first of the silver sands on the beach head, 'Well, that was easy m'lads; imagine them two just happening to be there when we needed them most. It's a pity Captain Kidd is not here to see this day but I am sure he is smiling down on us from Davy Jones's private Pussers rum locker and probably screaming in exultation.' Brassy and Grapeshot just smiled and shook their heads. The two not so jolly jacktars in question who were, of course, very much unwilling partners than willing volunteers had been press-ganged into becoming prisoners, or if they behaved nicely potential crew and who now had much time to reflect on their very ill-thought-out planned attack on Hastings, which was in itself a deception plan by Hastings where 'press ganging' was the art form of the day. Also, this chance encounter was not executed by mistake either as Hastings had been given vital information about the **man-map** from a certain lady who owned a watering hole called 'one eyed jacks', and the two scallywags were the remaining two sailors that had been **'inked'** earlier by Inkychung. The tattooist had acted as part of the cover-up and master plan originally orchestrated by Kidd himself, but sadly, earlier in the year, Captain Kidd had been detained under the orders of Lord Bellemont and was now very much dead thanks to the British Crown services and the employment of a very long length of rope and all the very important intricate detail of which was held by Mister Tee Chow the ship's cook.

And coincidentally, the master plot had been passed over to a select few after the untimely death of the ship's incumbent surgeon who appeared to have supped some doses of 'strychnine' as opposed to a good helping of the old Pussers rum and had somehow mixed the two bottles up whilst fumbling around in the darkest of nights for a drink, a task undertaken at the real dead of night. Sadly, Kidd had also joined the surgeon in pastures dead. One of the selected man-map groups was a man named Narender Sudaneni or Naru for short and had just been 'press ganged' by the Hastings gang and gun crew. This foreigner, Naru the sailor, was an Indian by birth and a man who was especially important to Hastings as he was supposedly the critical last and final piece of the complex man-map which also included a set of symbols and numbers captured in Anson's infamous log (The Horseshoe ledger or the map of Ubilla), and formed part of the small man-map that brought most of the jigsaw together. But to compliment this band of mapped gentlemen together, there was also another Mad Tribesman to be tackled and this man was called - Manoj De Mhal - who was the actual brains behind the two and he knew sooner or later that Captain Kidd or an associate treasure seeker would seek them both out and eventually bring the four men together to view the infamous map. Now whether the man-map group had any practical choice in the matter of this orchestrated encounter was an entirely different subject or question altogether. But in his infinite wisdom, Captain William Kidd at the time had somehow known that all four would eventually strike up an alliance of sorts and seek the treasure for themselves. Hastings had been made aware of the plan and had acted swiftly, and he also knew there was a piece of the map that indicated the final **'resting place'** of this mass of treasure.

CHAPTER SIXTEEN

'St Mary's Isle'

The island of Madagascar sits off the Southern east coast of Africa in the Indian ocean, and the population is predominantly Indonesian or known as the ancient Malagasy people. But as luck or serendipity would have it, just a stone's throw away across the small bay sitting adjacent to this magnificent place, there is an island outcrop known as **St Mary's isle** or Nosy Baraha, which is a lovely tranquil hide away covered heavily in mangrove trees and many other tropical flora and fauna. It was a very popular haven for merchant ships sheltering from the harsh Tsunamis or the horrendous typhoons and hurricanes that traversed these warm dangerous waters. St Mary's island, a long thin island that sits off the Eastern African coast, and became through time a good staging post for many vessels, albeit as its strategic location became better known, it also became a haunt for pirate vessels, which ultimately led to fewer ships running close to the Isle. Located on the island is the only cemetery actually attributed to pirates and for good reason as over one thousand have reported having been buried here, it was also not uncommon for the dead who had suffered illness such as malaria or typhoid to be buried along with the beach head nearer to the sea either. But, far as Pirate legends go, there have been many notorious pirates such as Adam Baldridge, Henry Every, Abraham Samuel to name but a few and had frequented the islands or had actually lived on one of the local smaller islands such as Ile aux Forbans in the bay of Sainte Marie's or the town of Ambodiffotatra itself. In the early 1700s, the French Colonials had laid claim to the island and it was not returned to Madagascar until late 1960. A mile or so west of the main inlet of the island sits a special spot known only to some as pirate's cove, where the heavy anchor of the merchant's vessel, the Adventure Galley, had just been dropped into the warm blue waters and had sunk deep into the soft silvery sand below. The location of which is where the vessel was to sit for a few days whilst remaining out of sight of marauding pirates or mutinous privateers but most importantly hidden from the British Navy who were on the look-out for quick booty.

Deep amongst the mangrove outcrop, a couple of hundred yards up into the thickest of forests, Hastings and his motley crew had taken their uninvited two guests along with their own man map crew and were venturing deep into a secret cave carved into the hillside. In the ensuing minutes, they had strung up the two aggressive pirates, Naru and Dhmal, together on a make-shift 'X' shaped frames, each man having been spread-eagled fashion and suspended near to a small river. However, the two Naval Gunners from the crew 'Brassy Townsend and Grapeshot Richards' stared on with a sense of anticipation whilst Mister Raddy Anka slowly drew a copy of each tattoo upon two pieces of large vellum and was busily joining up portions of the map together. Hastings was watching and acknowledged the ciphers and the symbols and gazed at what he knew was the star sign Taurus and recognised what he knew was the coastline of Chile with various numbers written along the bottom of the outline, then he spied the 'D' and then the 'M', but this time, he understood that these were Latitude and longitude references 500 and 1000, but kept quiet. Hastings smiled and then thought about the charts that Kidd had left behind him. After about two hours or so, Hastings viewed the parchments just as the ship's

Bosun had lifted his muskets out from their holsters and was about to shoot the two men dead. Hastings responded very quickly, 'What the hell do you think you are doing? The noise from the bloody gun-shot will ring loud across the island and bring much-unwanted attention. Now, put them away.' He barked in certain authority at the Bosun who was taken by surprise by the sudden outburst from the Buccaneer. He then responded, 'We cannot let these pigs live another day. They don't deserve to stay alive; after all, they were going to kill you back at 'One Eyed Jack's, or had you forgotten that already and that you would be worm food and very dead if Brassy and Grapeshot had not intervened. Anyways, we have the map now.'

Hastings nodded in agreement, waited a few moments, then walked in front of the two men and spoke very softly to them both, 'Listen to me carefully, I am going to save your lives this day, but you may have to endure a wee bit of pain first, a bit of discomfort, but trust me, that will be better than being shot in the head and dumped into the mangrove for the worms and termites to devour your heartless souls.' Hastings turned back to the Bosun and suggested an option: 'No, these pigs do not deserve to die, well they do, but not just yet. Although they will be punished nevertheless, even the good Lord above would forgive them for their manly charms under certain circumstances. And let's face it, after all is said and done, they are still sailors and obey our code. Let us prolong their agony and suffering. Let's face facts, shall we? Without them, we would never have discovered the secret maps as they stand today, and now we are so close to great riches, the 'Ophir of Solomon and unknown treasures in one strike', so I say rather than slaughter these two tyrants, let's remove their inks by fire. We can do this by branding them with a red hot iron to remove the tattoos forever.'

The Bosun started to lower both muskets and started shaking his head. 'S'pose another death would only make things worse,' he replied then casually walked away. Meanwhile, the ship's newly appointed surgeon had prepared a solid black iron horseshoe by fixing it onto a makeshift spike and was busy heating the implement for branding purposes in the hot coals. A single hot iron that was now glowing a lovely blood-orange-red colour waiting patiently to be used as an implement of certain pain. Hastings turned to the Bosun again. 'Well, Mister Bertie, have you the kind of stomach for melting the human flesh whilst it still has a beating heart?' The Bosun stared on and without a response, he continued to stare right through the Buccaneer as he spied a group of Indians in the far. Off distance, he smiled as he acknowledged that they were making their way slowly up through the dense foliage of the distant jungle mangrove pathway. He then lifted his arm and pointed as they were just beyond the edge of the rocky escarpment that led directly to the cave and then he then spoke. 'We had better make tracks, Captain. Those are not visitors, they are head hunters and they look bloody hungry to me.' Within a few short minutes of hell, confusion and mayhem accompanied by out and out panic, and crew of Pirates were soon taking flight and were ascending the high rocky outcrop and climbing quickly upwards to evade any encounter with the headhunting tribe. However, and very sadly in the chaos that ensued, two of the ship's crew had fallen to their untimely deaths onto the sharp rocks below. But all was not lost, depending on your own perspective; suffice to say that the head hunters may have captured one of the two spread-eagled sailors, albeit it was never really confirmed and remains uncertain at this time as one of the sailors was never heard of again, but we could say that since that very tragic day in the early 17th century, the local Indian tribe do enact a very special annual ceremony, and if rumours are to be believed, it is said that the islanders celebrate the cave offering to their God's by setting fire to two 'Skulls' that sit neatly on top of a large stone shelf that was neatly carved out of the ancient rock face. The first tribal ceremony ever conducted in the caves of the dead was led by their tribal chief arch head hunter, who was a man called 'Inkychung'.

CHAPTER SEVENTEEN

'The Avon Ascoti'

The crew of the 'Avon Ascoti' had donned their special night attire and had finished painting the tall masts and the copious amounts of rigging ropes with a heavy coating of warm black tar. Three very large iron buckets had already been hoisted aloft, having been stuffed with wood and horse hair, which had been washed down with copious amounts of pig oil... The Ascoti was on her monthly smuggling mission and was making ready for sail when the somewhat renegade British Naval Officer Captain Cornelius 'Fishwick' Webb stepped on board the vessel and made his first comment. Fishwick was a stout man of forty-six years in age and had been at sea most of his working life. He maintained a stiff upper lip at all times but harboured a very humorous streak that had often got him into hot water with the established Navy thinking. Captain Fishwick, having joined the Royal Navy ten years prior, since originally leaving Newfoundland on a merchant vessel that had sailed from the Barent seas to the West Indies and inadvertently as a crewman, was pressed ganged into service when by necessity he found himself working up through the ranks to achieve his current status as skipper of the Avon.

'My God. Man, she looks darker than hell herself. We will certainly be a sight for sore eyes when we encounter those Pirates head on. Those vile sea pigs will never know what hit them when we attack them full broadside. What do you think of that notion, sir?' he asked the First Officer who was standing nearby and was waiting for further orders. The first officer was about to answer the question when the Captain cut him short. 'No, young man, that was not a request to answer, it was a rhetorical statement. Now go about your business.' The Officer saluted and stormed off down the port side decks thinking that the Captain was another arrogant arse. The master plan for the Avon's crew was to engage pirate vessels such as the Quedagh Merchant, which had been a very long plan in its careful preparation for almost one and half years. Sadly, the inept British Navy office had failed to corner Captain Kidd or his crew as the merry band of sea slime were very aloof and the Admiralty wanted to bring them to justice rapidly. Albeit, the East India Company had originally wanted Kidd dead and buried and forgotten about a couple of years earlier, especially as he had almost single-handed brought down the company to almost financial ruin through his treachery as a pirate and his antics were becoming a great concern. The Avon Scotia project had been a secret plan invented by the British Navy and was simply designed for a vessel to only sail and operate at night; the master plan was for the vessel to intercept rogue traders and pirates and swashbuckling sailors twenty-four-seven, either attacking them whilst at sea or were sitting at anchors, and they often targeted more specific vessels which were used for raping the high seas, or specific vessels that the Admiralty had an issue with, irrespective of their country of origin. This plan also included torching many vessels whilst sitting at the dock in certain harbours in many countries across the known globe. The notion was to create a certain amount of fear amongst sailors who would literally 'crap their pants' on simply hearing the name of this fearsome vessel in any conversations. Therefore, over the course of several months, many wooden name markers were constructed and had been left at places of devastation where one will find that the nameplate 'Avon Ascoti' would be quickly found–having been strategically left amongst many a shipwreck debris in order to create the illusion that the Avon Scotia was present at all tragedies and she had been sunk time and time again either after a heavy battle or had simply run aground... Suffice to say that vessels encountered by the Avon ghost ship had never left their mark at any battle sites or left indication where they had been, but all that remained were the remnants of the ships destroyed carcass and the dead crew which would be highlighted to ensure that the message was being firmly applied across the globe.

That the 'Avon Ascoti' was bad news. The Bosun had started his jovial banter as the crew assembled on the long wooden decks. Almost every day, he would shout out many words and statements such as: 'Watch the mizzen mast, tie down the driver, and then the pusher, but here on board, we call them sheets, and they are not bedsheets, they are ropes, ropes, that if not tied correctly will fail and could cut yer head clean off. We have knots, bows, laces, sheet bends, cloves, and many more hitches to learn; we only tether those staysails and we watch for those gaffs; we must tie that spanker down tightly, and we always grab the halyards with strength and precision, then we pull the man up high into the mass of sheets and sales.' This repeating of naval sail terms was specially designed for the newer hands who had joined the vessel and needed to act quickly if they wished to remain on the crew.

The Bosun stopped for a few moments and gazed down at a broken wooden wheel spoke that had splintered around the concentric edge off the recess. He stared at the wheel again then shouted, 'Ships Carpenter to main deck soonest please and someone summon the house mouse to follow. Quickly, quickly.' He repeated again then stared directly at the young midshipman. 'Don't hang around young, sir, you have work to do as well; we have no time for fannying around like lost sheep; go find the large four-sided mainsail, then pull the complete sail and sheet to the desired position and shape her up if you will, and remember, step carefully, you hear? Don't underestimate those ratlines.' The Bosun tipped his hat and started his spiel once again, 'High end boom tip, gaff boom down, the deck area for scrubbing, ships rudder for turning, 'and the brig' is specially designed for you lazy sea-dwelling sea dogs and scallywags that don't do an honest day's work, and the brig, that is where you go if you get caught having holidays and don't take care of business. We must keep our vessel ship shape, and… we don't forget that we eat in the galley. We sail and navigate the oceans by the chartroom, and all our important decisions are made in the ward room.'

The Bosun continued his daily calling speech and simply waited for orders from the attending duty officers as he worked his magic across the decks throughout the day. The Avon Ascoti had sailed the high seas throughout the whole of the year 1698, although she was originally deployed to disrupt the ongoing efforts across Panama in a deliberate attempt to thwart Scotland's efforts to gain any commercial footprint on the international trading platform, but England and the Admiralty had other ideas in mind. It was around the same time as the Scottish trading company 'The Scotland Trading to Africa & the Indies' had been formed and the appalling clandestine secret unprecedented behaviour of the English was eventually designed from the onset to withdraw from their financial stake in the market when any negativity appeared on the horizon, and they quickly executed a plan that was, in essence, always designed to fail. But first, having been set up by the English Parliament with a 50% package on offer albeit, all of a sudden the English Government forced through a cowardice withdrawal agreement as the Spanish were also claiming that this was their home territories and had challenged the British crown to either war or debate, and very soon thereafter the King's agents very swiftly intervened and ran. But as many of the Scottish Directors had already sold many shares to ordinary Scots in order to raise primary funding for the plan, which took a deathly turn, and the project was already doomed to fail. The vision of utilising half of the nation's financial liquidity was communicated to have been placed in serious jeopardy. This idea and notion of misspent wealth was a certain myth as Scotland remained financially buoyant and strong throughout the campaign whilst retaining very substantial monies in her name to ensure a quick recovery from the ill-planned and ill-conceived very deceptive venture. The notion of Caledonia operating on the Caribbean coast of Isthmus of Darien was perhaps a certain pipedream but many other half-cocked projects have been hatched, but as far as the Darien project was concerned, we know today that the lands called Panama could have been under Scottish control and we are left with a dream and the notion of building a new Scottish future by anticipating the building of the great Panama canal having received lucrative insider information. And this was a warning for the future not to trust our English deceptive neighbours. In essence, it was at first glance potentially a very good opportunity adventure and was fuelled by the further potential of creating a full-blown city of commerce with complete infrastructure in place, which even by today's standards was completely fathomable in its context. It was a grand design that could easily sustain cities located up and down the Pacific coast. This city would require serious shipping and the marketeers to keep the world trade operating. The many advantages would be a fantastic trade route through to China via the Capes, and Scotland would benefit directly from the taxes and tolls applied to trade, monies paid for by the passing merchants. The plan was well-conceived and would have been a great achievement, but the final outcome was thwarted.

The first key point to raise its insidious head was the infestation of mosquitoes and the many infested swamps, and as a direct result, many crops suffered as a consequence, whereupon human disease was soon rife. The social impact of western settlers created another certain nightmare for the many tribal colonies that could have prospered but who were now at warring status with the new settlers and the Spanish colonies were also somewhat hostile. The situation did not improve in the longer term and over time hostilities reached peak level where the Scottish and Irish people were quite literally begging for not only food but fresh water, and we have learned through records the people were denied any support under the English Kings direct Orders, along with no further humanitarian aid. As a distinctive mark of failure and poor management, coupled with lack of any humanitarian support from the English King empirical records show that over two thousand people had died unnecessarily and with these poor souls on land and the several ships that were also lost at sea or remain unaccounted for were a sad revelation.

The social and economic impact had greatly affected Scotland and of which would be a very stark historical lesson to live with. Albeit one thing was very clear in the hearts and minds of the Scottish Nobles and their people was to never ever trust English politicians, ever again. However, operating in the back drop of this monumental failure regarding the Caledonia experiment, the merchant vessel, the 'Avon Ascoti', had served her clandestine purpose in her short tenure having already sunk several merchant ships in and around the coastal ports of Darien. The project itself did not bankrupt Scotland but certainly came at a high cost to some entrepreneurs who had speculated, and the sheer conjecture that their drive for riches almost collapsed Scotland's finances is pure myth and fantasy, again communicated by the deceptive English media classes and people such as Anson, as they tried to discredit Scotland and her many forward-thinking endeavours, and the British crown operated as an insidious political reptile at work coupled with copious amounts of political negativity trending and campaigning that Scotland or Caledonia will witness and endure throughout its turbulent history up into this very day.

CHAPTER EIGHTEEN

'Ophir - Solomon's Ethiopia'

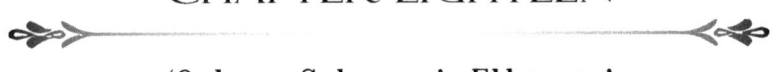

T he mistress of the sea, The Adventure Galley, and her crew had once or twice in her early days circumnavigated the treacherous waters in and around the area near Afar in Ethiopia where the crew had made several overland journeys across the areas of the Northern territories as they gathered jewels, animal hides, and copious amounts of coffee. The land itself was said to have been where the Queen of Sheba had once lived in the hinterlands of a place called Axum and held a seat of great power over her Queendom. The modern-day Eritrea frontline was certainly a dangerous place for any visitors and scholars or indeed would-be treasure-seekers who dared to venture deep into this volatile backdrop of a desolate land, and more so in this modern age; therefore, as a direct consequence, great care is taken by the local government to ensure that the 'relic' known as the Ark of the Covenant, which is said to reside and highly rumoured with great authority to contain the original ten commandments from biblical days, is still held as a national important subject. The Queen of Sheba, a known icon of the old world, who may also have had two very important names applied to her status with regards to Egypt or conversely, she may have been known as Queen Nefertiti a great Queen and had married King David and subsequently gave birth to their son Menelik. A man who in his lifetime had documented many travels to and from the Holy land, and on one such visit was purported to have saved the Ark of the covenant from relic raiders and false idolaters and brought the holy ark relic across the desert lands back Tana Kirka or to Axum. Today, the relic is protected by ancient and modern Levi monks and clerics. The capital city of Ethiopia is a city called Addis Ababa, which retains records that state that the Ark and other holy relics were brought into Ethiopia a thousand years before the advent of Christ and have remained there up until this very modern day. According to many legends and the physical Ship's Log that George Anson had left behind, he had stated that the Coastal area of 'Afar' was translated in the Egyptian language a colloquialism for Ophir, and could be a form of slang at that time which was alluding to an area which could have been pronounced as Ofir or 'Ophir', literally meaning the area of Afar.

From many other maritime explorers, we understand that the Horn of Africa is a very rugged landlocked country split by the Great Rift valley where we will find that the village of Aksum or Axum is the location of a once-bustling huge colony, albeit today the land comprises of great obelisks, tombs, castles and the most famous church known as 'The Lady Mary of Zion'. In this modern age, The biblical Ark of the Covenant is said to be hidden here, which, in essence, is the ultimate holy relic depicted as a gold-covered wooden ornate chest that carried great secrets, and according to some Levite Monks, the Ark holds the original Ten Commandments given to Moses by the almighty himself. The additional artefacts of interest within the Ark were also Aaron's rod and a pot of manna and the tablets (Tabot), which were all present at the site of the biblical Mount Sinai. And there was the additional furniture from the Tabernacle to consider, sitting amongst the many letters and documents that Hastings had illegally borrowed from Anson from the HMS Wager, there included three parchment letters, one of which was of letter of warning written in Latin Greek and broken English; it was supposedly written by the ancient Levite themselves, albeit the English text was added by persons unknown, these ancient prophetic scribblings contained the message about death, and the deathly warning to those who chose to ignore this ancient illuminated text from biblical history. The Levite note basically stated that those men who choose to interrupt the way of the Lord and interface with the Holy Relics of the 'Tabernacle' who have not indoctrinated into the secret methods and procedures required to be in the presence of the Lord will be judged and most likely killed by the awesome power of his holiness.

Hastings in his presence of mind certainly thought that the warning was certainly stark and clear, and he was going to avoid any contact with the furniture of the Tabernacle at all costs, then took a moment to pause thinking about the candle holder. 'Well,' he thought, 'the relic has not killed Kidd or the crew so far, so perhaps we are safe for now.' The additional briefs held a single note from one Captain Henry Morgan simply said, 'I fear the mystery of the Ophir'; her gold and ancient treasures may be of bountiful fortune but alas! The booty is protected by a hellish force (The Black Lodge) in the form of a sea-going vessel that is not of this world, and that devil ship was the 'Avon Ascoti', a fearsome pirate vessel sent by Lucifer himself which has shadowed our every movement over several weeks.' In another one of his personal accounts, the ship's log had an inscription that: The vessel had also been plagued by the existence of this shadowy entity and said in his notes: 'We have already encountered the Avon yet again, although she never came any closer than five to eight leagues, but it should be noted that before we docked in a small port in Ethiopia, the ship from hell had sat off our port bow for nearly six hours and that was several days ago, albeit she was as quiet as any cemetery.' The vessel master was quite clear in his summation of the vessel and its movements, although he never really explained as to why the vessel never attacked them; however, after five days of anxiety and nervousness, the crew of Anson's vessel who were tired and simply hanging on a knife's edge had begun squabbling and fighting amongst themselves. The Captain knew and understood the men needed much rest as scurvy was beginning to set in, then one day the Avon was suddenly gone. She had vanished out of sight, pulled her anchors, and disappeared as quickly as she had arrived, sailing stealthily into the warm mists during the night.

The Adventure Galley crew on reaching the lands of Ethiopia had also intended to march overland to seek marketeers and trade for the infamous holy relics they had heard so much about and were then going to head out Northwards to the gateway of Eritrea to the great canal that ran up and beyond the mountains and into Egypt. The master plan was to meet with a few foreign marketers at the crossing point known as 'the crossing of souls', which is a junction crossroads that either led a person deep into the central mountains to meet thy fate or Eastwards into the valleys where anything can happen to both strangers and locals alike. The strategic trade routes were simply the ancient goat and sheep tracks that crossed over several paths near the borderlands of Northern Eritrea and onto the shores. The crew had almost completed a four-day march and then returned the remaining part of the journey via river boat to the Eastern mouth of the wide estuary, which was a great relief to the crew, and eventually sailed South and joined their ship. During this expedition overland, the crew had met with several tribesmen across the terrain and traded with them whilst employing their ranks as both scouts and guides and were telling tales of biblical treasures and the wealth of the great Queen Sheba. Landing at Ofir was not a first option as intended at the port of Afar but the skipper was literally forced to sail onwards and eventually dropped her anchor three days journey Eastwards across the coast nearer to a place known in Arabia a small inlet near the straits of El- Mandeb on the Red Sea. The vessel had remained in the dock for a further four days then had set sail to another small port to meet incoming traders at Ezion Geber on the Red Sea at a place hailed as the land of Edom, then sailed from there on to Afar in Ethiopia. After their trading was finalised and the inland adventure completed, the vessel then sailed back to the warmer waters of the Caribbean, albeit she was still being shadowed by the Avon Ascoti from a distance.

Kemp Hastings recalled that he had been conversing with Kidd and had quietly raised the question regarding the menorah. 'Where did you get it?' he asked as Kidd looked up from his desk and spoke, 'Get what?' Hastings grimaced a little. 'The menorah. That huge candlestick or whatever you want to call it, the one in my cabin. I fell over it last night, nearly broke my neck. It's just that I think that we are probably the most unlikely vessel afloat that would carry or possess such an important holy object if it is indeed the real thing.' Kidd had just stared into the wilderness beyond his desk then responded, 'So, obviously, it's a relic and probably worth a fortune, but where did it actually come from?' Kidd had stood up and very slowly walked to the window with both his hands tucked behind his back. 'Before you joined the crew, I had set up a meeting near the coast of Chile with an old acquaintance from within the East India Company about eighteen months ago, and he showed me a place on a map that was so important that twelve men had already died whilst trying to acquire this treasure map. That map was a plan of a small island sitting just off the coast of Chile and this place was called Juan Fernandez. Now Fernandez was an explorer from the last century and he was a great explorer, and rumour has it that he discovered great riches in Peru and he had quite literally robbed the Inca people of their wealth and beliefs. However, Fernandez also was purported to have taken stock of some holy relics and gold that was known as the Temple of Solomon artefacts, and he apparently had acquired a few select pieces and had stashed them with his other 'loot' near this island.

Now the land area around this archipelago in Chile is covered with volcanic mountains and, therefore, the islands were a great place to find locations and many smugglers' caves to use as drop points for cargo. Somewhere, along the timeline, the Knights Templar under the French Marque had met with Fernandez and acquired many pieces from the explorer and returned them back to the Templars. As it appeared, Fernandez had also discovered unknown sea routes between Callao in Peru and the city of Valparaiso in Chile, and now we know that the known location this Juan Fernandez island was named after him and sits in the South Eastern Pacific Ocean about three hundred miles from Chile. Although the man, Juan Fernandez, was pursued and chased for many years, he had always evaded capture, hence, why they called him the witch of the pacific.'

Hastings was quietly nodding and had been reacting to the skipper's body language and remained silent. 'Now whilst in Peru, I was press-ganged by a Templar crew from the vessel the 'Temple Unicorn I,' and was unceremoniously thrown into the brig, but it was not for long because the Captain of that vessel, one Lieutenant Adam Duncan of the Royal Navy, had stepped in and made my freedom bid on my behalf, but that was at a price, and he knew of my existence and my nature. He told me that every pirate vessel on the seas were after his ship and that the vessel was going to be scuttled somewhere off the Barbary Coast, and he had also told me that if I wanted to live any longer, then I would need to do some work for the Lord above. He also requested a great favour and because I had access to the most cut throat crew next to hell, I was then tasked. But the upshot was that I was also paid in gold to deliver a single piece of cargo to Ethiopia. And that deed is done and my debt to Duncan is paid and I was also told never to reveal the coordinates of the vessel whilst it was in Chile.' Hastings had recalled the complete conversation and thought that perhaps he should meet with the same people Kidd had done eighteen months earlier.

CHAPTER NINETEEN

'Kidd's Eternal Grave'

As a tall man appeared to be walking carefree between the many old gravestones, the sun broke the clouds and shone over the dishevelled cemetery. A single block of grey stone caught the eye of Kemp Hastings as he kicked a few small stones across the pathway. The stone slab in front of him was two-foot in height and two-foot wide and had suffered through time as mother nature had shone her hot unrelenting radiant sun over the land. Albeit, on the odd occasion, would send torrents of rain down on the 'shadows graveyard' across the small island of the Saint Marie landscape and had done so for centuries. The gravestone itself had been slightly sheltered by a larger epitaph that sat directly behind it and of which had provided a large shadow for at least a few hours a day. In reality, the shadow was quite literally preserving the rear façade of the slab. Hastings spied the writing but noticed that 'no name' actually appeared on the front of the stone and was simply inquisitive as to why in the late 17th early 18th century anyone would pay handsomely for a grave plot and a headstone but have no inscription or name of the interred person etched onto the surface.

Hastings thought the slab was facing the wrong way as well and had deduced that perhaps it had been reinstalled the wrong way facing back to front, or had been reset after falling over or had been deliberately placed in the ground this way, who knows. He carefully stepped between two other gravestones and bowed his head as he passed Captain Anderson's headstone, another dead person who appeared to have been a shipping merchant and who had died in the year 1621, and another interred Seafarer called Cap'n 'Ted Teach' who had recently died in March earlier in the year. Hastings stopped and momentarily appeared to have a huge grin that slowly swept across his face; it was more of a grin of bemusement than anything else. He turned his head around and gazed over the cemetery and beyond the large gateway. Removing his hat, he took a very deep breath whilst filling his nostril cavities with the warm smell of sea air and sweet roses. Then spoke softly, 'You clever man, mister Kidd. You very deceptive, unruly, untrustworthy old scoundrel. I take my hat off to you, Mister Captain Kidd.' Hastings read the back of the headstone, and it read:

- **Oro Ut Omnes Sequantar Viam Ad Veram Vitam'** - 'I pray that all may follow the way to true life' find **DM.**

The inscription was etched across the top arch of the stone, but what made him smile was sitting at the base of the slab. He had observed that sitting within a small oblong cartouche the word – **W.K.I.D.D.** had been etched in one-inch high lettering. The world at large knew that William Kidd had swung from the gallows in London in 1701 and was hung and slain as a pirate. Therefore, why would anyone want to find his grave on a foreign Island so far removed from the British Isles? But Hastings had known the true secret of the man map for a long time; he also knew that Kidd would have a second back up plan, and he also knew the lettering and numbers he was searching for were supposedly inked on the soles of the feet of a woman, a person who was no lady either, and she was certainly no good wife, but the daughter of William Kidd was indeed a very good candidate and a lady pirate. Her name was Willemina, and she would live on an island of the Saintly lady of the biblical Marie, and that could only be Saint Mary's in Madagascar and, of course, Kidd himself had ensured that Willemina (Mary) Kidd was protected as a pact between him and the old Captain for as long as he could. And now Hastings was about to meet the lady in question, Willemina K.

- 16.8944 degrees South 49.9059 degrees East - The island.

As his mind started racing, the young officer removed the old ships log from his leather satchel and flicked through the pages for several seconds, and then stopped and stared at the page in front of him, running his finger over the top of the vellum he began tracing the lettering: **DOUOSVAVVM. Willemina aka** Mary K had started a career as a local trader in Madagascar, rumoured to have been sponsored secretly by William Kidd. However, this relationship was a very private affair indeed, and as the young Willemina would be an easy target for unscrupulous bandits and, therefore, he would have to be careful as they would instantly kidnap her and put her up for ransom, especially if it was common knowledge that she was related to the infamous William Kidd. We can acknowledge that during this golden age of piracy that many such women had left their homes in order to take up new professions that brought money into the household and put food onto the many bare tables. On the odd occasion, females would turn to piracy and simply dress as men in order to join the rank and file of marketeers or buccaneer crews, and some women had started companies that sold their ill-gotten gains and booty with absolute discretion, and their product was either supplied by reputable people or had been quite literally stolen from the many questionable cargoes and spoils of high seas booty that made it to the island of St Mary.

Willemina was somewhat fortunate that her young husband had died of malaria early in the 1700's and had not convicted of piracy or had he succumbed to the discipline of law, and she was permitted to continue trading as the innkeeper of the local tavern 'One eyed Jacks', which was previously her husband's responsibility, and Willemina was also fortunate enough to have inherited the complete property. This life provided her with a fair amount of freedom for the young widow, albeit she never remarried but continued her business empire with not only the public watering hole being a good source of income, but also running the local pawnbrokers shop which would deal with not only the local gentry but also cater to the passing trade that set foot on the island. It was not uncommon for Willemina to not only hide the business transactions of her clientele but also hide the clients themselves who were more often than not pirates. Willemina would say that her job was interesting and paid well, and her circle of friends may have included figures such as Anne Bonny or Mary Read infamous female pirates, hence, why she took the nickname Mary to join the trait of the female pirate legacy of St Mary's island. Hastings located a few scribblings on the page and then read the small passage that sat neatly in the margin of the ship's log.

'Heaven and hell our ancestral spirits, the classical underworld,' he muttered as he flicked through the pages.

- 'I have left - the planet I am the way, the truth and the life'.

After all these years of searching, Kemp Hastings had quite literally returned to his religious thoughts and very early teachings. He was never a true Christian believer and he would be the first to admit this, but somehow, the tides had indeed changed, and yet again the Latin lettering had resurfaced in another piece of work. Even after all the years at sea chasing dreams and false promises, he had quite literally found the reason that he had been looking for. And had only gone to the cemetery to pay his wishes to some old departed colleagues and ship-mates and to pass some time before he sailed yet again into another adventure, but he had not reckoned on being so surprised in doing so. Hastings recognised the Latin phrase instantly, – '**Ego sum Via et Veritas et Vita**'.

And as he viewed its script, he knew for certain that this had clearly been written in the hand of George Anson as he had seen it often enough. The inscription referenced the biblical book of John, but like most conspiracies, Hastings knew that they the establishment and other unscrupulous bastards wanted the Holy Grail or the cup of life. But had Hastings really inadvertently stumbled on the resting place of the chalice amongst other Holy Relics let alone the cup that once held the blood of Christ, or had Captain William Kidd once again set another misadventure for someone to follow and eventually be disappointed? Hastings stared once again at the gravestone with the intention of coming back at the dead of night and digging up the grave of a man who that he knew was not there. But what had Kidd left behind and why would he have purchased a plot and tombstone if he was never intending to use them? All very weird as far as Hastings was concerned, but then again, Kidd was a somewhat complicated man; perhaps he did bury a treasure or a piece of history still waiting to be discovered, and was he a man that would do that kind of thing? Hastings thought, *yes*, and lay the ship's log down by his side on the soft sand and leaned up against the gravestone of the pirate who was not there whilst taking time to day dream.

As Hastings took a few minutes to nap in the hot sunshine down in the village, a young lady had locked the door to 'one Eyed Jacks ale house and had started making her way up the long winding path leading toward the pirate cemetery. She was carrying a few flowers and a flagon of ale, and as she reached the old iron gate, she spied the bulk of Kemp Hastings, sprawled out over the gravesite appearing not to have a care in the world. She walked slowly and carefully and as cautiously as a cat hunting a mouse as she crept up on her target, albeit taking her time not to alert the pirate as she advanced to the near kicking point. Then she spoke softly, 'I hope you are comfortable lying there in the sun. Not very respectful sitting on someone's grave, you know.' She paused and waited for a response. 'Indeed,' retorted Hastings as he slipped his hat up over his brow. The girl responded in a harsher tone, 'As the ghost of that particular pirate will come and haunt you until your dying day.' She spluttered in an almost angered repose. Hastings twitched a little then turned over to face the maiden. 'That may well be true, my fair maiden, but highly unlikely as this particular pirate was hung in London in 1701, so you will have to do better than that if you want to frighten me away from here by ghostly stories because I am really here simply to meet you, and believe you me when I say that I know this because I was there when they hanged William Kidd esquire and he also told me a few things before he was taken. He says you have 'Blessed Feet', so the question I may need to ask you is: Who are you, what is your name, and what do you have in common with William Kidd? Are you a lover, a friend perhaps, a niece, mmh perhaps not, but maybe a daughter? Hence, why you have brought flowers here on this particular day, his birthday, as they surely are not for me.'

The young girl took another glance in his direction, gave an impromptu smirk, and kicked the dust from her shoe and the pathway in his direction. Hastings stood up. 'No need to get in a tizz young lady, I am not a threat to you, nor anyone else for that matter. I have no desire to desecrate this grave or create any ill-feeling either, as I did know William Kidd very well. I have sailed with him for a few years on the Quedagh Merchant and the Adventure Galley. I also saved his life as well, although he never mentioned much about his family, well, apart from the wife. But he was very protective over that subject unless you were, Tee Chow or Raddy Anka.' Or those two great apes that followed him around. He had replied hoping that the mention of old crew names might trigger a distant memory in her head. By her reactions, it had. Hastings continued, 'I know that Sarah Bradley Cox was his first and only wife. Sadly, I never met the good lady, but I can presume that Sarah is either your mother from one of her past marital acquaintances or that Kidd was your father. It matters not to me which one because life has to go on as they say.

'If William Cox had not sadly drowned or John Ort had not died so young or so long ago then we would not be having this conversation, now would we?' Hastings rubbed his chin and smiled again. 'I know Bellemont was a complete bastard and turned on the family before the trial and I was not aware that Bellemont and Sarah's friendship had failed so badly either, albeit I did hear that politically Bellemont had also taken his share of bribes and payments from some unscrupulous people and had simply distanced himself directly from Kidd and any of his affairs in order to escape any accusations of treachery or money issues. And I know one hundred percent that he had hidden the important 'Letter or Marque' from the lawyers, and Bellemont never presented the letters themselves to substantiate any support for the Captain during the trial. And the reason I know that fact is because I am the current owner of that exact letter and it came directly to me from a servant that served at the Bellemont estate. Before I met William Kidd, he had apparently worked closely with Lord Bellemont who had financed many excursions and expeditions on his behalf, and he had quite literally financed ghost journeys to dupe his colleagues and partners out of more raw cash in the process, his problem being that he had also roped the King of England into the deal. But why Bellemont had Sarah arrested and imprisoned, then accused her of piracy affiliation, was beyond me, until you realise that Bellemont used Miss Sarah as bait to get to Kidd into the country in order to arrest him. But, sadly afterwards, Sarah Oort Kidd was now tagged as a criminal as well, and although she got her private possessions back, Bellemont had, in reality, ruined her life at that stage. I was personally enraged that it took two years to get the trial underway and that the legal process should have been an open and shut case with Kidd being found not guilty and exonerated from all charges. But those charlatans at the Admiralty, and in New York those self-serving political corrupted bastard whigs. They were all in this sordid affair together and may their souls rot in hell.'

Willemina took two steps back and glared at him. 'I do know that was the story in the public domain but there is a far more serious side to this Bellemont than you know, Mister Hastings. Sarah Bradley, my mother, had also moved many stolen articles around the island, but when we first lived on the island, a friend of Bellemont had set up residence and was spying on the tavern visitors and many other people of interest in the community for ages. Well, it was said that someone had killed this man and threw him in the sea off the southern cliff, and Sarah knew who this person really was, but she would never tell anyone. Although back then she had married William Kidd and he was a well-to-do man and she was finding her new life very comfortable, of which Bellemont was to become a very big part of it, as he was an important figure in society. But to lock her up in jail for a few weeks was not a good thing to do, especially for an innocent person in this affair. But today she struggles with her many failed marriages, and she now lives quietly out of sight from everyone.'

Hastings chose not to ask any more questions but had a soft heart spot for empathy regarding the life of Sarah Kidd. As the two newly discovered friends walked along the beach, Willemina had stumbled forward and Hastings had noticed how delicate of a figure the girl actually was. She was fresh, in her late twenties, and possessed a wild sense of adventure and humour. But he spied the two tattooed letters on the bottom of her feet when she lifted her legs and that was when he suddenly stopped fooling around and stared into the wilderness. Willemina, sensing that he had changed his mood, very suddenly splashed him with sea-water. He nodded his head and thanked her for the splashing before commenting, 'Your feet... did you know you have writing on your feet?' The girl stopped in her tracks and wiped the sand from under the sole of her right foot, then commented, 'Of course, I do. My blessed feet. They are my own feet; it's my birth date, or so I am told, but I can only see them with a mirror. It's also on my other one too. Here, look,' she said, lifting her leg and falling over backwards into the soft sand.

'Can I look at them both?' he asked. 'Of course, you can,' she replied, then sat back in the soft sand and placed both her feet together for him to see. Hastings started to smile again. 'So, you were born 'D' and 'M 1500', were you and again on the 'CLXXX' - 'VOVV'?' She replied instantly, 'Yes, but I can see it only upside down; it is in the year 1680 on a MON-day, well that's what I was always told, so I never really thought about it. So, what are you thinking about, Mister Hastings, do you find this strange?' she asked then decided it was not really relevant to ask him about her date of birth and obviously she did not possess a dastardly highly educated complex and deceptive brain that would stoop to such low levels of deception that one could quite literally hide the whereabouts of a billion dollars haul of treasure, especially cleverly by tattooing the location on to your own daughter's feet. But then again, if you're Captain William Kidd, this was his kind of logic that perhaps only he understood best and would normally be an unthinkable context for most people. And to Hastings, it meant that Kidd knew exactly what he was doing with the Man Map and had laid a plan so cunning that modern-day cryptologists would find it difficult to crack. The man map was a ruse, it was deception, albeit Kidd had informed Hastings about the Island and his daughter during their time together before Kidd was summoned to meet his maker.

Willemina Kidd stood up and then brushed herself down of sand. 'It is not really my father's grave, Mister Hastings, it is mine. W. Kidd stands for Willemina Kidd. My mum was told by Kidd to bury his belongings in his grave and Sarah at that time thought that it was a great idea, and after the Captain was politically murdered, well, she also knew that the world of piracy as far as she was concerned would go quiet after a while, and, therefore, having hidden the rewards that were brought back from his last trip, she knew they were going to remain safe, and she moved away for a short time. Although Kidd was not sure what was happening in his absence whilst at sea, actually, he thought that he was acting in total legality with the Letter of Marque served by King William the IIIrd to him and his cohorts, but he had no idea that he was being systematically set up by Lord Bellemont for not only the murder of William Moore but additional piracy charges on two other occasions, and a contract with Lebanese and Armenian partners within the East India Company.

CHAPTER TWENTY

'The Demise of the Avon Ascoti'

The '**Merchant** slipped her moorings both quickly and silently and was in the process of making her cannon of fifty-two ordnance pieces made ready and was preparing for engagement with the infamous Avon Ascoti. Captain Kemp Hastings had received intelligence that the Avon had been anchored near Holly Cove, just off the Southern coast near to Madagascar, and that the vessel was apparently being prepared for war but was planning to be moored very near to the British Naval Fleet and was deemed to be planning and joining the attack towards the many incoming merchant vessels. The crew was now preparing for the most important face-to-face battle with one of the most frightening vessels that supposedly ruled the seven seas under the cloak of fear. Hastings had gathered the crew together and explained the real story behind why they were going to engage the Avon: to kill the myth that this vessel was under a dark mysterious entity but it was really just a normal vessel that was employed by the British Navy to reign fear over all the potential ships she would encounter. He explained that the vessel was designed carefully to demonstrate that she was on fire and was still sailing under normal sail, and then he went on to explain the true 'political murder' of Captain William Kidd and he held the Certificate of 'Marque' and had shown the crew. 'Gentlemen, when Kidd set sail to New

York, he intended to meet with Lord Bellemont and reconcile our position whilst gaining a legal pardon from the British crown in order to ensure that we as a crew could continue to operate as a privateer vessel. But as most of you now know the skipper was 'press ganged' by the yanks and imprisoned until he was sent to London and quite literally hung for treason. So, now that we have returned to Madagascar to face an enemy that may well outnumber our crew and cannon, I ask that you keep your faith and loyalty to one another, and once we defeat the 'Avon Ascoti', we will become free men. And I will also tell you this right now, the vessel, the Avon Ascoti, was once named the 'Degrave' and she was found grounded. The British renamed the vessel, taking the name of the Nova Scotia, but that was not a good idea considering many vessels that sailed the seas from Canada may be confused as to their country of origin, but then they changed it to the Avon Ascoti, so you see, my brethren, that this vessel is not a devil ship, she is simply a marketeer pirate vessel run by the British, and that makes her fair game for us to attack. So, as I said, we will destroy her first chance, and then after the deed is done, we shall sail to our next location and drop anchor for the very last time.

'As you know, since our journey back from Arcadia - Nova Scotia, where we encountered the many ships moving the Scots and Irish to Canada last year, but let me remind you men having dropped off our very religious Holy Relic at Mahone Bay, then as far as we and Kidd are concerned, we have done our duty. And, I will say, gentlemen, you should all fully understand that this was a very important journey indeed. And that the Holy relic was called the Holy Menorah and a candlestick that illuminated Solomon's Temple, the very place where the Stone of Destiny and the Ark of The Covenant were stored. This is God's treasure as mentioned in the old testament. I think together we have no real idea how important this journey was, but it was for God via the Holy Order, and we have preserved history, my friends. These Relics will now be secured and hidden for eternity within Oak Island under the custody of the Miq Maq Indians, and the Holy Order.

'This mission was from God as our departed skipper would have put it, and it was his final act for clemency perhaps designed to appease his God, and hopefully, he now rests in peace. Captain Kidd was very angry when I spoke with him on many opportunities and he was more annoyed and perplexed that he had misread the attitude of the day regarding Bellemont and those parcel of scoundrels at the East India Company and Bellemont, who was by definition using his spouse Sarah from 'One Eyed Jacks' as sea bait and she was duped like the common fish to entice Kidd back to the Americas, and we all know and understand that as a result, he was captured by the authorities under the secret orders of Lord Bellemont. And I know that he was more upset that he took 'you' men, his crew, into certain danger, and for this act of deception, he blames only himself for this because when we were in London just before his death, he told me many things. And let us remember that he took this secret to the grave with him and that secret was that of the Cara at Catalina – and the Quedagh Merchant, and we should all make good as a crew on his eternal wishes once we destroy the Avon Ascoti. So let us raise our swords and charge your muskets; prepare all the cannon with full monkeys of shot, Brassy, Grapeshot. I want your best efforts. I want the crews to run the cannon decks like clockwork, and, gentlemen, when I hear '**Fire in the Hole'**, we will be launching great fire balls of shot, and we will be firing them high into the night sky until we are done, to ensure that we burn that devil vessel in its entirety. And then we will burn it to its last remaining burning ember, sending it swiftly to Davy Jones's locker, no quarter, no warning, and no second chances.'

Hastings continued to engage his crew and raised their motivation of undoing all the many wrongdoings they had suffered over the last three years, after all, they were about to attack the best prize of all a British Naval vessel and put their lives on the proverbial line. Hastings raised his cutlass into the air and shouted, 'Gentlemen, let me inform you all that Kidd's liaison with Bellemont and the plunder of the British East India Company was very deliberate, and as a company, the East India Company is now in certain turmoil and almost in ruin, and that is due to Captain William Kidd and his crew who were undoubtedly responsible as was myself, and we are all charged with treason as together we stole the many cargoes from the East India Company directly under Captain Kidd's approved letter of Marques, and we all have a debt to pay, as we were all part of the plundering forces and yet we took it from right under their very arrogant British noses as they traversed the open waters.

This constant upheaval and dis-array were mainly due to this very crew's unrelenting pillaging campaign as we had targeted all opportunities of the many merchant ships that served the markets, and subsequently, as a direct result, the EIC company had declared us all as outlaw pirates and are using all their political clout to get us all arrested whilst pushing for the death sentence to be conducted soonest. So, gentlemen, as a final order and mark of respect for Captain William Kidd, I intend to attack the **Avon Ascoti** in the early hours of tomorrow morning, and we will attack and destroy any other British or foreign vessel that comes within a few short cables of our bow.' Soon thereafter, the Merchant sailed out of from her moorings in the early morning mists and found the Avon sitting at two hundred yards off the coast near the bay and appeared to be asleep; her blackened masts and uprights dominated the night skyline as the skeletal shape of the squared rigging silhouetted against the prevailing light. But as far as the Quedagh was concerned, the Avon was a sitting target.

As they sailed closer to the frigate, there was slight movement observed on the upper deck as a single sailor and a watchman had started to raise the alarm. The watchman started ringing the ship's bell, but it was all too little and far too late as the Quedagh had already shot a massive volley of twenty-four cannon toward her broadside and the heavy firey shot struck the Ascoti midships, destroying the main mast instantly and the gun deck in the first strike, then all hell was unleashed as a second volley of fireballs found their targets, including the vessels hold and forward mast, which instantly caught fire and a series of explosions ensued.

The crew by this time were seen to be abandoning the ship en-masse and were swimming ashore to save their own lives. The attack was quick, silent, and horrendous and the Avon was taken by total surprise and skill, especially as the Captain and his officers of the Avon had taken leave of the vessel earlier that day and had met with their peers and other Officers on the island. It was a meeting that had quite literally saved their lives, and sadly as an indirect consequence, left the vessel under the semi control of a young officer who had succumbed to the wishes of the crew and had himself partook in a few yard arms of pussers rum, and opened up the perfect opportunity for an attack. After only twenty-one minutes, the Avon had been sunk and was now embedded into the soft sand just off the coastline of St Marie's Isle. Hastings tipped his hat backwards and smiled, although he appeared somewhat sad that he had destroyed one of the most feared vessels that had sailed and attacked the ships of some well-known Pirates such as Edward Low and Howel or Spriggs, albeit the Navy had failed to capture their foes in any of their conquests.

Kemp Hastings remained mindful that the people who had carried out the Admiralty's orders had also been complicit in torture and murder of innocent people, and he acknowledged that these serving Officers would simply join one of the Admiralty's other vessels whilst continuing to wreak havoc for legitimate privateers who operated under a 'Letter of Marque'. In his ship's log, Hastings had written the following: 'The Avon Ascoti now destroyed was not the British Admiralty's finest twenty-one minutes. Once the aftermath of the Avon had settled down, the Quedagh Merchant remained on station ensuring that they would remain there until the main mast and the carcass of the vessel had burned and removed from existence.' Hastings had ordered the removal of the ship's name plate the 'Quedagh Merchant' and had it thrown overboard and knew that it would eventually wash up onto the beach head to ensure that the external world would know that she had been in the area. Hastings would also rely on the survivors to tell the external world that the 'Ghost of William Kidd' had returned and was taking revenge for his murder.

CHAPTER TWENTY ONE

'The Sword dedicated to William the IIIrd'

As the vessel was making headway away from the island of Madagascar, one of the ship's crew had reported to Hastings that three barrels of pussers, a pig, a goat, and a sea chest had been observed floating from the scene of the watery and fiery carnage. Hastings ordered the recovery of the booty and requested that the chest be brought directly to his quarters. After cleaning the burned embers from the lock and hinges, he became alert that the chest was not of normal construction, as it appeared to have far too many nail heads or retaining pins protruding around the circumference of the lid. 'Mmmh! I just wonder if this little chap has a surprise for us.' Tee Chow watched on very bemused as was both Gunners Grapeshot and Brassy who were slowly easing their way closer and closer to Hastings as he pulled the chest towards himself but turned it around with the hinges facing him, then he removed his scabbard and began prodding the locking mechanism with extreme caution. 'Gentlemen, this is a Spanish arms chest. I have seen these before and they are very dangerous; they have little knives hidden in secret compartments and they will cut off your fingers or your hands if you are not careful.' Hastings twisted the knife in and around the workings of the lock and jumped slightly as he heard a loud click that released the mechanism. Hastings took up a position standing over the back of the chest whilst placing his hands on the outer edges and slowly raised the lid. After a few seconds pause, there was another loud snap when the chest went 'Kadunk' and seven small sharp blades sprang open and would have certainly hurt or cut unsuspecting fingers that would have normally been placed at the front of the chest if it was opened normally. 'Wow!' yelled Tee Chow. 'Rat not norrymal, kood cut finger off, velly nasty, velly, velly nasty.' The two Gunners Grapeshot and Brassy did not really do much as they had expected as much from the Spanish and knew these foreigners never played by the rules and would resort to such nasty dirty tactics, pretty much like the British.

Hastings thanked the crew and then opened the sea chest and delved into the abyss of paperwork and clothing. He pulled at a large book and caught his right hand on a metal object that was sitting diagonally across the bottom of the box; he then slowly felt his way around the bottom of the kiste, eventually grabbing what he thought was the handle of a sword. Extracting the blade from the chest, he gazed on in bewilderment whilst observing an older rusty piece of blade with a very ornate hilt, and then held it fully upright. He smiled inwardly, thinking that the Captain had most likely hidden it away out of sight as a reminder rather than using it as a killing implement. Laying the sword down on the wooden floor, Hastings satisfied himself that nothing significant sat at the bottom of the box and stared at his hands. 'Once again, Kidd, you have imparted good knowledge to me that has most likely saved my hands and fingers this time.' Hastings then found a bottle of Pussers and broke the seal. He had noted that the sword had an unusual inscription written down the full length of the blade and commented, 'Now that's not common; don't often find such weapons with that type of etching around the place. I wonder why the Captain of the Avon Ascoti kept this weapon in particular; maybe it belonged to a friend or family member, or it was one of the many acquisitions and loot that the crew of the Avon had already relieved in their tenure as pirates from one of its many victims.' Hastings gazed for a few moments longer at the steel and decided that it was such an elegant ancient weapon to be just sitting around in an old sea chest and obviously appeared to be an important relic in itself. The pirate would be the first to admit that his command of the Latin language was very poor indeed, albeit he struggled to understand all of the scripts on the sword, and then took a very rough guess at the inscription that had been etched on both sides of the blade.

He burped out an impromptu laugh and looked over the sword, realising what he thought it meant. *'I wonder if old William had been mugged by the British empire before he was made King.'* And what an irony just thinking yet another Scotsman and potential King no less was being elevated into the muddy ranks of the Monarchy of the British. Is this really what this sword highlighted? He wasn't sure but was certainly amused. He thought that the actual text was quite specific and then translated the inscription in his mind again.

+N D X O X C H W D R G H D X O R V I+

'Omine Domini XOX (the Trinity) Comes Hollandia Wilhelm (II) Dei (gratia), Rex Germania (et) Hainault Dei (nutu) XO (Christus) Regnat, Vincit, Imperat'

+ In the name of the father, son and Holy Ghost - (The trinity) - Count of Holland William III by the Grace of God – King of Germany a Hainault by the will of God – Christ reigns Conquers and Commands+.

By any definition, swords were obviously very personal Templar weapons and were always deemed both a weapon of war and an instrument of worship. On the one hand, the sword was a killing instrument highly effective for butchering and killing aggressors, whilst at the same time the sword blade was also a personal 'altar' when the blade was pointed earthwards, sharp end first, forming the cross of Christ; it was not uncommon for swords to have very personal inscriptions on their blades or haft, and on some examples they had small cross pate symbols etched across their killing surfaces. It should also be noted that captured within many Templar documents, they do describe an act of self-salvation that as soon as practically possible after a battle had ended and the bloodshed had ceased, a Templar Knight would kneel in obeyance and thank God for sparing his own life during the course of the battle, but they would also pray for the souls of the unfortunate people that they had just slain in the face of adversity, and a Templar Knight would raise his sword high, reaching into the sky, and ask the Lord above for forgiveness.

Hastings had been to the Holy Land in his earlier years as a Knight of the Crusade but had never experienced the art of killing people on such a mass scale as the crusades were. Of course, he had encountered the odd foe, albeit he knew that there were secret laws and obeyances that he himself simply had to obey. As he read the wording on the blade, he took stock of the fact that he had already deciphered part of the complex structure of Anson's DM Code to think about, albeit was not very enthusiastic about having to make sense of yet another one; that fact alone would simply send his head spinning and get his brain bent out of shape as all the bananas that he had encountered in the Ivory Coast in the earlier years. In real terms, the sword was forged for a King of the early days, but the real question was: what was the real meaning behind the inscription? And the obvious rationale with most scholars was that the script was either Latin with Greek influence, and perhaps a splattering of shortened abbreviations alluding to feudal religious beliefs, and that the swordsmiths adapted 'idiosyncratic symbols' and specific words that could have stemmed from the same workshop. These early forgings for a Templar Knight were a deliberation and would have related to ancient mystical Christian authority mostly driven by the Crusading Orders through the

13th century. Not dismissing the cross pate either as an important symbol; however, like most Christian symbols, they are easily recognisable by most of the religions across the middle east, albeit the five-fold cross of Jerusalem was not so as readily identifiable as other Orders of which they would have displayed on their mantles as this red symbol which depicted the five wounds of Christ.

The etchings down the blade of the weapon was a clear message to those receiving the sharp end of this blade, and would certainly be embedded into the last thoughts of the victim as they gazed onto the cold steel of a Damascus edge. As a mark of motivation, one would have been driven by faith having cleaned, prepared, and viewed their swords before they tackled their foes.

CHAPTER TWENTY-TWO

'Telescope'

On returning to Saint Marie's Island, Hasting had met with Willemina and shared a few quieter moments at the empty graveside of what should have belonged to Captain William Kidd. The girl appeared to be disturbed and was contemplating something that made her quiet and somewhat distant. Hastings leaned over the lair whilst resting his arm on the Epitaph stone and smiled. 'You look very distant this morning, young lady, have you lost your way in life, or has the beer gone off at the tavern?' She smiled back at him with a lazy smirk and brushed her hand through her red hair before commenting, 'No chance of the beer going off, it is always off. Captain Hastings, my father, was a pirate, but he was not an angel and he was certainly no saint, but I am sure that he had taken someone's life for whatever reasons, although for the most part, he did ensure that my life here on this little island was made safe and secure and he had let it be known to all men that should any harm become of me or my friends, then he would return and torch every last house in the village and bring this island to the ground he had also supplied me with a fair amount of wealth over the years and had returned every other year on his birthday. But when he had my mum, Sarah, he dug this grave on my behalf and erected this stone just four years ago. He never really spoke about why he did that. Sarah Oort knew but she would have found it all too macabre to discuss in any great detail as she had buried three husbands, but moreover, she stated that he would probably need it shortly after what she was hearing in the many rumours that had circulated New York. She said that the lair will keep a secret that every man will die for, and that certainly won't be for the bones of an old pirate. I remember that it was during a really bad rainstorm that Kidd had arranged with a few friends to dig the actual grave with soft sand and had packed it with lots of coconut leaves and some tree bark. There is, from what I know, a real coffin is in the hole. Kidd says that it was his last belongings as long as he was 'alive', and that they were never to be touched unless he was dead. And now that he has gone and Sarah had dashed off to the big city life, well, I can see no other reason why we should not to dig up the box and see what they had buried and left behind in there.'

Hastings looked a little confused before commenting, 'Certainly is very odd that a man who was still alive would have a grave dug on his own behalf in the first place unless, of course, it was for the very good reasons and that he was, after all, a pirate and held a penchant for hiding riches across the continents in strange places, but the question we should be asking is: Are you the only person apart from Sarah that knows this great secret or was this secret shared with any others? Myself being an example.' Willemina took a step backwards and nodded her head to the left, then responded, 'Well, we will only know that fact when we dig the box up or when someone else comes looking. After a few hours of discussion and a few ales later, both Hastings and Willemina Kidd returned to the grave and had recovered the somewhat heavy-laden coffin. Together, they could not physically lift the thing out of the ground. The box had been interred only three foot down and was by all accounts an easy dig. On opening the coffin, Willemina extracted a rounded long box that appeared to be in the shape of a ship's telescope or spyglass holder. Hastings looked on, started laughing out loud, and fell backwards down on his bottom, shaking his head. The girl was a little distracted and amused but stared on nevertheless. 'What are you laughing at?' she asked, placing the lid back down on the coffin, having acknowledged a few other special large gold and silver items that were neatly packed together in the casket. She had kept the idea of returning later to investigate, as she was already starting to burying the box again with her bare hands. Hastings then piped up.

'Willemina, stop and take a few minutes, no one is going to disturb us at this ungodly hour, but I would wager that the contents of that spyglass holder are a vellum document or a map. I just knew in my gut that Anson or Kidd would have hidden something so important in a very simple place, or, in this case, a spyglass holder, an everyday maritime instrument, an implement that will be used frequently, and a bloody telescope case of all things—brilliant thinking.' The Willemina unscrewed the lid off the container and extracted the spy-glass and a vellum scroll approximately one foot in length and one foot in width and it was indeed a 'map'. It was not just any map, but it was a very colourful, detailed map that any man would die for, according to Kidd, and was written in several languages but predominantly in Latin. She passed the parchment across to Hastings as she took the end off the telescope and started to look out to see. 'Damn, it's not working!' she exclaimed, then passed the scope to Hastings who took a quick glance through the spy glass in jest and then suddenly muttered a few incoherent words: 'That's because the lens is broken, but I can see, wait a minute… I can see some small letters on the inside. It is someone who has actually etched Roman numerals along the inner brass plate inside this spyglass.' He then read the letters out loud: '**XXXIIIXLIIII – LXXLVILX**'; therefore, I guess this is another map reference that Captain Kidd has stuffed some of his loot. Maybe he wants you to go find it.' The young girl smiled. 'Well, as things are at the moment, I think Kidd wants us both to go find whatever it is he has stashed there. And how did he know that this would happen?' Hastings looked through the glass again and then picked up the vellum parchment, acknowledging that it was a very well-drawn chart depicting a region in South America, Chile perhaps, and there were the references to a location cleverly etched into the spy glass.

Hastings then spied that code, which he was just becoming a little too familiar with from the onset of his adventure, again, albeit he possessed a very limited understanding of alchemy and he would struggle to decipher the map on his own successfully, although he could understand that there were fixed star signs and zodiac influences with what appeared to be ciphers written in Spanish and thought that it was pretty basic maritime knowledge. He acknowledged many biblical references alluding to the Temple of Solomon and the Middle Eastern countries. He already knew that the Holy Menorah was safe in Oak Island as he himself had taken it there and handed it over to the Templars Knights and the Miq Maq Indians. He then paused for thought, thinking upon the notion that Kidd may have actually found some of the many other great riches of the ancient biblical temple or had the actual Templar map or a copy of it. He then ran his finger over the symbols again, acknowledging the many images of the Holy Trinity and absorbing the maritime symbols denoting islands, sand depths, white beaches, rocky outcrops - Ebanin (rock), and then he stopped staring at the map and looked around the cemetery before speaking. 'Willemina, this is a treasure map of South America, which looks like a map that does appear to indicate what I can only see as references to the stars and biblical treasures. And, we definitely cannot ever let anyone know this is here because if we do, then we could both end up dead rather quickly.' Willemina just smiled and stared back at him and spoke softly, 'Okay, but there is something you should know, and that is: do you know who those guys are?' she asked whilst turning and pointing to three pirates walking up the cemetery pathway. Hastings slowly placed the map in front of him. 'Here, put the map back in the box and don't say a word,' he said whilst standing in front of her to obscure what she was doing from the oncoming men. They turned swiftly and spoke, 'Where the hell have you lot been? I said meet me at one eyed jacks watering hole. But it is good to see you.' Hastings then turned around and introduced Willemina as a friend who was helping him with finding accommodation.

CHAPTER TWENTY THREE

'The Horseshoe Expedition'

In the years that followed the life of General Juan Esteban Ubilla, who was a naval mariner and had been tasked to hide immense biblical wealth, we should acknowledge that there have been many global treasure seekers, including the British and Spanish governments, who have chased the greatest hoard of wealth imaginable in human history for many years. The latest excursions being the journey of a British merchant vessel called 'The Unicorn', commanded by a Captain Cornelius Webb who had embarked on what was to become known as the **Horseshoe Expedition,** in order to discover the great wealth of King Solomon and the Incas whilst operating under the directions and orders of Lord George Anson himself. Albeit as the expedition was unfolding, Anson had sadly died in the year 1762 before discovering whether or not the wealth was ever discovered, leaving a great deal of uncertainty and conjecture as to what has happened to the riches and the treasure map. Even more importantly in the latter years, the two very important 'letters' between Captain Webb and Anson, and a special code that highlighted map references **'D' and M'** being the start point and first recorded reference to the DM Code itself, and the first reference captured in any correspondence which had triggered the journey coordinates being somewhere in and around the Cape Horn.

Subsequently, the so-called Royal Orders were opened by Webb, and of which quite literally directed **the observer** to the secret entrance and the goal of the project, which should effectively lead to the discovery of at least several hundred barrels of gold and silver and many Holy Relics or the wealth of Solomon, including sixty chests containing trinkets, rings, necklaces, goblets, gold, and silver chain and many statues caste in gold. However, as the good Lord above would have it, the Unicorn suffered a violent storm and the ship lost its main mast and was damaged beyond its sailing capability and was, therefore, forced to shelter at '**Lat and Long'**, near to the Valley of Anson and one cable distance from an observation post near **West Valparaiso**. According to Webb's last letter to Anson, the letter also included a few references to issues that had occurred during the expedition, and that was after a short time the vessel **Pinnace** was seconded and the Unicorn destroyed by a fire deliberately by Webb to ensure that it could not be refabricated or used for pirate purposes, and that was the last detail up until in 1761. However, destroying the Unicorn had also involved murdering the six crew that had remained on board to keep its sordid story secret. Kemp Hastings had recalled that one of the items he had stolen from Anson so long ago was what he thought was a few early planning notes of his infamous journey or an impending voyage around the globe, and those also contained a map regarding the Juan Fernandez Islands and of which Hastings himself was convinced was a similar outline map that he had traced in Poussins oil painting, albeit in feint detail. Hastings checked his own notes and showed Willemina what he had been scribbling in his notebook since joining Kidd on this so-called biblical campaign over the last two years. He recounted a reference to the **Cerro tres Puntas'** or an action which would close three points, but in reality, he still had no idea as yet what that meant; it could be the middle of a triangle. Then there was the 'Cara', which was this Island of Clara near Chile, and as opposed to Cara in Catalina, he was slightly confused as he had so many notes and certainly knew that any map could be false along with other notes and diagrams, not forgetting the Tattoo inscription and diagram 'that Tee Chow' had drawn as part of the man map. But from his memory recall, sadly, there was still a few spaces on the map he had to fill in, even more so missing middle piece of the tattoo which should have captured a series of numbers or letters denoting exactly what Captain Kidd was alluding to, and that critical part was still hidden.

Was it really the location of the **'Cara' map** and the gold booty that was held on board the Adventure Galley at the time? Or was it the directions to God's very own signature pieces that Lord Anson and the Admiralty knew existed and had embarked on the Horseshoe Expedition in order to acquire great wealth? But they were clearly overshadowed by the Knights Templar and the Priory of Sion, who were not quite ready to permit any unscrupulous marauding half-cocked government to steal the wealth of King Solomon from their clutches, as this was in essence 'Templar Treasure', and that meant that it belonged to the Vatican and no King in his own right mind alive was going to challenge that authority of the church unless of course if they knew the future outcome of King Henry VIII and his opposing ideas, which had actually turned the status quo 360 degrees on its head. And quite literally, he, as King, had ex-communicated the church from his mindset, especially regarding the church and biblical treasures, which made perfect sense that many avenues of misdirection were already at play in order to protect their wealth by employing some very ingenious ways. Kemp Hastings was a very neat writer, but when he was just scribbling things down swiftly, he would write as if he had dipped the quill in a spider's nest full of ink and scribbled the words down that to him almost made sense but in a haphazard fashion.

'Peru paradise of the sun, Asmodeus the Christian protector of holy relics, beware of chests that have booby traps – knives and broken glass. King Solomon the Davidic line to Solomon's Treasure, Was Sofala or

Zimbabwe the Ophir? Kebra Nagast the holy bible of Ethiopia – glory of the kings. The island of Juan Fernandez, the archipelago Chile, find General Ubilla y Echeverria at Mas ateirra.'

The daughter of Captain Kidd on the other hand was not so convinced that all his writing was jibberish; after all, she ran a pirate tavern that housed scallywags pirates, cutthroats, deviants, sailors, fisherman, and the worst kind of all Navy Officers who knew everything about nothing, and she had heard many a story and many a tale that had led to great riches being discovered. But, for now, she wanted to walk in the warm water along the beach and Hastings had agreed to walk with her but only for a mile or so, as it was getting hot and he had to find some new crew for his next excursion to somewhere near Chile.

CHAPTER TWENTY-FOUR

'Santa Clara Island'

Sitting in the Pacific Ocean off Chile in the region of Valparaiso, there sits an obscure tiny island called 'Santa Clara', which is located near to the larger group of rocky outcrop isles that make up the Juan Fernandez islands and archipelago in their entirety and firmly set in an idyllic time stopping backdrop of volcanic mountains. The isle is located only one and a half kilometres South West of the main islands, and its landscape predominantly flat with rocky escarpments reaching no more than three hundred and seventy-six metres in height. Santa Clara hosts a range of smaller beaches across the islet and mariners should be careful when negotiating the islands, even more so when approaching the Southern tip as an ocean geographical anomaly in the shape of a long deep sandbar sits just under the water line and is interspersed with a smothering of sporadic sharp rocky outcrops that would rip the timbers from the hull of any ship in no time should a vessel stray near or too close to the coastline, especially in bad weather. Santa Clara has an overall area mass of around two kilometres and is a haven for wildlife such as goats and feral rabbits, coupled with a range of fauna and flora, teaming also with a healthy mass of both weeds and shrubbery. Hastings was taking time to keep the vessel moving slowly across the reef as he approached the island from the South knowing full well that this style of marine terrain was not just treacherous but very dangerous. He was looking for a specific flow of lava located in an inlet and ironically also in the shape of a horseshoe; it was a geophysical anomaly that had formed several million years ago, and that was according to Captain Kidd who stated that a sloop such as the Adventure Prize with a flat keel could easily squeeze between the natural underwater 'valley' or 'slip way' and would be pushed by the incoming tide into an inlet only four hundred yards long, then the ship would run aground onto the soft sand. It would then be necessary to drop anchor and keep the vessel fast and stable because as the ebbing tide turned, it would quite simply pull the vessel back out to sea. Hastings was still quizzing his notes when he was disturbed by the Bosun. 'Skipper, forward bow lots of rocks, but there is a reef that might just be this causeway thing. It's sitting just under the water line, half a man depth, and I think we should drop anchor and wait to see what happens if this is the valley. Then I can also see a horseshoe cliff face from the bow.' Hastings smiled and stood up. 'Excellent, Mr. Bertie, don't drop anchors just yet, we will 'bring a spring upon her cable' and then we will back the beast up onto the sand.' The Bosun stuttered for a moment before speaking. 'But, Captain, we might wreck the rudder.' Hastings had a very quizzical smirk on his face. 'That may be so, Bosun, but we need to 'careen' the stern and the hulls as they need cleaning from barnacles, and besides, I want to be able to escape in haste if we need, but trust me, we are certainly not getting crimped by the British or any other scallywags today, so let's get ready. 'Handsomely' heave to Bosun and see if we can negotiate this channel; make it so, Mister Bertie, if you will.'

'Aye aye skipper,' came the prompt reply as the Bosun headed back off toward the Foc'sle.

Hastings placed the telescope to his left eye and smiled. 'Got ya.' He then muttered a few odd gargled words as he spied the co-ordinates on the inside of the lens. After 4 months at sea, they had reached the final destination that Hastings would call his last adventure.

- 'XXXIIIXLIIII – LXXLVILX' (33 42 11 - 78 56 60).

As the Adventure Prize slowly eased its way into the underwater channel aft end first, the Bosun was calling out the draft heights and watched as the vessel simply ran aground. After a few minutes of scraping the soft sand below, the Adventure Prize was becalmed in the sand.

Hastings and the two gunners along with the Bosun and Tee Chow, accompanied by Willemina, the ship's newly acquired surgeon, stepped down into the soft sand and slowly made their way to the wooded copse on the shoreline and then sat down. Tee Chow was first to speak, 'Capitano, how you know where to find this place? It is no painted on any map I ever see, velly clever, velly clever indeed.' The Bosun was next to comment, 'Tell me, Mister Hastings, are you telling us that Captain Kidd had this map all along and yet we spent two years waiting to get here?' The two gunners just stared on and remained quiet. Hastings then provided an answer or two. 'Gentlemen, the man map was indeed a real treasure map but it was not a map to gold and silver, it was a map leading to a gravesite and that grave belongs to our dear Willemina. You see, gentlemen, Captain Kidd had suspected something was not right and therefore took many extra precautions to keep his plan secret, and part of this deception plan was that he hid this particular location and map embossed into the spyglass case and the instrument. This was the map that he acquired from young General Ubilla and he had them buried in a grave on Saint Mary's Isle, the very same one that you, Tee Chow and Brassy, found us sitting near a few weeks back, and that was the grave that Captain Kidd had acquired. You see, when you put the man map together, it only took you as far as Madagascar, and the missing pieces in the middle were another map of Saint Mary's Isle, and the missing numbers, well, that was the difficult bit until I spied the lovely Willemina's feet. You see, before Kidd died, he had told me his grand plan and that I was to go find the grave.' Tee Chow looked very bemused and started laughing. 'Capitano, I think you say 'feet' I not hear rightly.' Hastings interjected, 'No, Chow, you are right, you did hear me correctly. I did say 'Feet' as Kidd had tattooed a code written in Roman numerals on to the feet of Willemina here, but that was when she was a young girl and has actually walked around with the secret location of this very island for many years thinking that she had her 'date of birth' tattooed on her own two feet, hence, why Inkychung and his head hunting friends would never have found the island, or indeed this place, the Santa Clara Isle, as Kidd had intended and had arranged things that way. But then I think Captain Kidd was even cleverer than I had given him credit for, as he had also taken the broken spyglass from the Quedagh Merchant and had managed to have the map references from the Ubilla map also etched in Latin along the inside of the scope, and you can only see it if you looked into the glass. So tell me, who would want to look into a broken spyglass? Anyway, I was trying to work out this DM Code thing and try to establish where all the loot was and the location of Kidd's wealth.'

The assembled party just stared on in bewilderment and struggled to find the strategy and logic in Kidd's thinking, let alone as to how Hastings had been so clever to work out many things, but it boiled down to Kidd telling him most of the answers. Willemina suddenly bent over, took off her shoes, and showed the group her feet. The Bosun leaned over and politely asked if he could wipe the sand from the bottom of her feet, and in doing so it became very clear that the letters were quite evident and written in small Latin letters - 'XXXIIIXLIIII – LXXLVILX'. Willemina then said, 'And this, gentlemen and lady, is the final destination and location of our intrepid journey. Welcome to the Island of Santa Clara, and that island over there is Juan Fernandez island. This is horseshoe bay and what I think may well be the resting place of some greatest riches ever discovered and hidden from prying eyes, and the resting place of God's secrets. Well, folks, that is according to Captain William Kidd.'

Grapeshot and Brassy looked at each other and instantly spoke in unison, 'Madagascar.' Hastings laughed loudly and threw his tricorn hat into the air shouting, 'No, gentlemen, not Madagascar, but here on the island of Santa Clara. But without getting to Madagascar, we would have never have found this place.' The Bosun then posed another question, 'So where is all this treasure then?' Hastings stood up and asked both Gunners Grapeshot and Brassy to stand up. He then pointed to the tattoo on Grapeshot's left shoulder which depicted a 'Horse-Shoe' then also pointed out that the island was also formed in the shape of a seahorse. He then asked Brassy to show him his right shoulder, and there was also a tattoo depicting an 'Archer'.

Hastings commented further, 'Well, folks, we are sitting in the middle of horseshoe bay and we can look up into the night sky and see many stars, however, for the last eight days we have been following the star of the 'Archer' to this very point, and I can tell you all that sitting to the left of that rocky escarpment over and up a bit, there is a cave entrance which is covered with foliage, but we cannot enter the cave yet until the water level drops and we can cross the river that ebbs so we can find the stepping stones, as the mud bed is covered in deep silt or sinking sand. And, folks, that will be later on this evening. And when we enter that cave, we will have to reach down under a long ledge and crawl through an opening, which will bring us into a large cavern that houses the riches that we have spoken about. Here, you may find many things, including what people are saying could be the body of Mary

Magdalene or Christ. Hastings reached into his satchel and pulled out the poussin sketch that had triggered his sense of adventure and explained to the crew what he thought, that it had been a simple painting with a map etched within the subject matter. But coupled with the Templar vellum parchments, Kidd's sketches and the seven maps and letters received from Captain Esteban Ubilla and some sketches from the Anson theft, Kemp Hastings was reasonably assured that he had hit the mark straight on the 'X' and all that remained for them to do was simply cross a muddy ditch and find a cave that sits within the valley and enjoy the riches of serenity and peace.

In the early hours of the morning, five vessels had arrived through the dead of night and Captain Esteban Ubilla had somehow followed them into the Chilean waters and had waited very patiently for the 'Adventure Prize' to return and try to claim a 'booty' that was never to be found by anyone other than the Knights of Malta.

END

AFTERWORD

George Anson' died in the year 1762; however, his secret DM Code remains in the public domain to this day, still waiting to be eventually deciphered and laid to rest. In his tenure, Anson had indeed been involved in the mysterious legacy of the Inca treasures and the Davidic temple treasure trove. There were many rumours that Anson left several notes and papers behind him and if they still exist, then they should also lend a hand to corroborating the reality of the 'Horseshoe Expedition', which in itself was an adventure resulting in the murder of six innocent sailors who were quite literally blown up by Captain Webb in his drive to keep the location of the sunken Unicorn a secret, whilst simultaneously attempting to hide the entrance point to the bay and caves where tremendous wealth may lay. As a murderer by his own volition, Webb, according to his letters, had sent to Lord Anson, but he was never brought to justice for this dastardly deed and should have been treated no differently to that of any other unruly scallywag pirate of the day. But the British establishment had turned a blind eye and protected Webb, albeit, conversely, when it came to dealing with Captain William Kidd and his sentencing, the British establishment took no time at all and turned their coats, then went out on several limbs to ensure that Kidd was politically brought to justice and eventually murdered by the establishment under the shadow of the crown, having initially been jailed in America, then unceremoniously delivered to the British as a high seas pirate. Although with hindsight, Kidd was an appointed Officer possessing a Letter of Marques for operating as a privateer on behalf of the British Government signed by King William and coupled with the staged event of mutiny brought on by Gunner William Moore, who had sadly died as a result of his actions mainly due to a blow to his head from a bucket thrown by Kidd to save himself from harm.

But, unfortunately, Moore suffered a fatal injury and never recovered, hence, thereafter, Kidd was deemed a murderer by default. Charges were lodged and brought to light not only by the establishment itself but also by Lord Bellemont who failed to support his colleague because Kidd had targeted the East India Company in his endeavours as privateer acting on behalf of the British Crown, as it raped and pillaged its way across the known globe working (under the arrogant, British colonial mindset that built and lost an empire). Global relationships were at a low and Bellemont had clearly wanted to remove himself from any political relationship or affiliation with Kidd or his crew and eventually extended his wrath towards Kidd's family and wife, Sarah, who was imprisoned for a short time at the behest of Bellemont. Kidd had attacked the Armenian ship, the Quedagh Merchant, which was by all accounts a partner in trade with the British, and the assault on its flag had become a political minefield, and Kidd was to blame as he decided against the rules regarding the use of the letter of marque. India had become insulted and the King of Britain had to act swiftly if international relationships were to be maintained, therefore, an example was to be made on the international stage and Captain William Kidd was the 'Lamb to the slaughter.' However, once Kidd was arrested, his spouse, Mrs. Kidd, was released and her belongings returned. Although in reality, Bellemont had used Kidd's wife as bait in order to lure him back into the country where he could have him arrested and subsequently charged for both treason and murder. Anson's papers, which added substance to his book (A voyage round the world), alludes to the great project in question known as 'The Horseshoe Expedition', which subsequently refers back somewhere in time to correspondence between Captain Webb and Lord Anson discussing certain details of the whereabouts of the infamous Davidic Treasure Trove, which appears to have been embellished with an insert of a 'spurious map' scribed in the manner that related to Juan Fernandez Island.

One could argue that certain aspects of the map in reflection was an outline within the Shepherds Inscription, using secret geometry, and could be engineered to fit the Shugborough relief if you wait long enough and convince yourself that it does. The author intimates that many copies of maps were made, especially when the art of misdirection was the tactic of the day and also reflected Templar Traits throughout history. Of course, we should remain sceptical when maps suddenly appear in older furniture or found in old sea chests from the 17th century 'era', which may well contain exact copies of maps and could lead the would-be treasure seeker to great riches. However, the **caveat** is that knowledge and corroboration do go hand in hand, and remember that Kidd's Letter of Marque, if presented, could have saved his life, although it suddenly turned up after his death.

AUTHOR BIOGRAPHY

Andrew has written several novels around biblical history mainly in an around the existence of ancient institutions and clandestine organizations, his most recent work Ophir was written whilst in Lockdown and focuses on the old world Pirates of yesteryear, with the addition on historical events that are as potent today as they were in the 17th century.

Andrew enjoys fantasy writing that is based on truths and would be the the first to admit that every novel consumes his everyday hours with research to source the many facts that are built into the fine tapestry of his storytelling.

'Every novel is a journey of discovery'

Lightning Source UK Ltd.
Milton Keynes UK
UKHW022043060722
405471UK00005B/433